Foiled

Second Edition

Foiled

Second Edition

Mike Faricy

Library of Congress Control Number: 2023914845
paperback ISBN: 978-1-962080-17-0
e-book ISBN: 978-1-962080-18-7

MJF Publishing books may be purchased for education, Business, or promotional use. For information on bulk purchases, please contact the author directly at mikefaricyauthor@gmail.com

Published by

MJF Publishing
https://www.mikefaricybooks.com

To Teresa

"Come here to me now till I tell you."

Acknowledgments

I would like to thank the following people for their help and support:
Special thanks to my editors, Kitty, Donna and Rhonda for their hard work, cheerful patience and positive feedback.

I would like to thank Ann and Julie for their creative talent and not slitting their wrists or jumping off the high bridge when dealing with my Neanderthal computer capabilities.

Special thanks to Ann for her patience.

Last, I would like to thank family and friends for their encouragement and unqualified support. Special thanks to Maggie, Jed, Schatz, Pat, Av, Emily and Pat for not rolling their eyes, at least when I was there, and most of all, to my wife Teresa whose belief, support and inspiration has from day one, never waned.

One

We were out on Angie's deck sitting in the hot tub, just the two of us. She was a petite little thing of Korean ancestry with jet-black, shoulder-length hair, flashing brown eyes, a delicious little figure, and weighed no more than a hundred and five pounds. That said, I'd met her at my karate class, where she was the instructor. She'd proven on more than one occasion she'd have no problem using me to clean the floor.

We'd been in the hot tub long enough that I was almost through the six-pack of Finnegans Hoppy Shepherd. It's a pretty good beer, so actually, it hadn't taken all that long. I opened the cooler to grab another and realized there was only one left. Then I noticed Angie was still on her first, and as a matter of fact, not even halfway through.

"You're having another?" she asked.

I'd just opened the beer, and the satisfied gasp from the bottle had apparently caught her attention.

"Yeah, I mean, with all the hot water and the jacuzzi, I have to stay hydrated," I joked and took a sip.

She shook her head. She'd been doing that a lot lately. After a moment, she gave a long sigh, like she'd suddenly come to a momentous decision, and stood up. I immediately did a thorough scan of her gorgeous body and set my beer down, ready to welcome her with open arms.

"I'll be back in just a minute," she said and climbed out of the hot tub. She grabbed her towel off the chair and just threw it over her shoulder, not bothering to wrap it around her, a fact I appreciated. I stared as she walked into the house and disappeared from view. She was back two-thirds of a beer later. She stepped onto the deck, grabbed a lawn chair, and dragged it over to the edge of the hot tub.

"You got any beer in the fridge?"

She gave another long sigh, then grabbed the belt on her terrycloth robe and cinched it tighter. Just in case I missed that not-so-subtle hint, she turned off the jacuzzi and the heater. "We need to talk," she said, then sat down in the lawn chair and tightly crossed her legs. Any sense of romance basically evaporated. Past experience warned me that any time a woman said, "We need to talk," it was a safe bet the conversation wasn't going to go my way.

"Dev, you can be really fun… sometimes. No offense, but I'm looking for something a little more stable and a lot more permanent."

"Two words not too often applied to me," I joked.

"I'm aware of that," she said, not seeing the humor. "I thought with a little encouragement, maybe some direction, God forbid a modicum of discipline, you might change. That now appears to be a distinct *im*possibility…" She went on from there, backing up her hypothesis by listing example after example for the next forty-five minutes. I was out of beer. My skin was all wrinkled and prune-like. The hot tub where I'd been relaxing was now just lukewarm. I wasn't sure if I should hit myself over the head with an empty beer bottle or just slip beneath the water.

"…could be really sweet, but I don't want to hang out in bars night after night. Your dog always eats my thongs. It would be nice sometime to go to bed and, I don't know, maybe simply talk about how the day went or something."

"Talk about how the day went?" I didn't get it.

"You know what I mean, Dev?"

Actually, I didn't, or maybe I really did. "So, do I know him?"

"What?"

"I'm guessing you've met someone, and you find him a better fit than me. Right?"

"No." But she said it in a tone that made me think I'd hit a nerve.

I climbed out of the hot tub, grabbed my towel, and wrapped it around my waist. "Give me a minute to get changed, and I'll get out of here."

She just nodded as I slowly made my way to the door, waiting for her to offer an alternative, maybe continue the 'discussion' in the bedroom. She didn't make the offer.

I made my way into her bedroom, pulled on my shorts and t-shirt, slipped my sandals on, and turned off the bedroom light. I peeked out the corner of her bedroom window and watched while she sent a text to someone. At a quarter to twelve on a Wednesday night, I guessed she was letting whoever it was know the deed had been done.

I turned on the kitchen light as I went back out to the deck, alerting her to my approach. Her phone was nowhere to be seen when I stepped onto the deck. "Angie, I'm going to take off, I…"

"I'm sorry, I didn't mean you had to go," she said, then stood up and hurried toward the front door.

I attempted to catch up. "Yeah, I suppose I could hang around and talk about how the day went. But if I hurry, I can get down to The Spot before close. You sure you don't want to come?" I said, then gave her a kiss on the cheek. "See you around."

She held the front door open, and said "Goodbye, Dev, it's been…interesting," as I went out the door. I hadn't taken three steps before the lock snapped shut behind me. I hopped in my car and hurried down to The Spot.

TWO

Morton was in his bed next to my desk, busy working over a new rawhide toy. I'd been studying the girls in the third-floor apartment across the street from my office for the past thirty minutes. Something was up, they had two sleepover guests, possibly sisters. All four of them were in thongs and curlers, sipping champagne, eating coffee cake and applying makeup at just a little after ten in the morning. There must have been music playing, because one of the girls was shaking everything she had while another was singing into her champagne flute and making moves like she was playing Madison Square Garden. At this rate, they'd be lucky if they were still on their feet by noon. I bet none of them were interested in talking about how their day went. I thought about going over there and of-fering encouragement.

I turned at the sound of someone knocking on the door frame, Morton was too involved with his rawhide to notice. She looked familiar, maybe, but I was blanking on a name. Maybe an even five four, blonde, blue eyes, nice figure, and silver earrings that dangled a stone. Di-amonds, I guessed.

"Hi, Dev, long time no see."

I recognized the space between her front teeth. Bonnie Lowry, from Climax, Minnesota, if I recalled correctly, and given the name, who could forget? I always thought the space between her teeth was cute. She was right on the money with the 'long time no see' remark. I'd met her at a wedding a good ten years ago. A guy I knew had married her sister, Chrissy and Bonnie had been a bridesmaid. She'd first caught my attention standing up on the altar in her bridesmaid's dress, light blue if I remembered, although the dress wasn't what had attracted my attention.

The butterfly tattoo on her back certainly wasn't the only tattoo among the bridesmaids. They all had ink. It's just that Bonnie's butterfly happened to be a well-endowed, anatomically correct, naked woman with butterfly wings. It shouldn't have been surprising, after all, this was a theme wedding, Jack Daniels being the theme. It was one of the few weddings I'd been to where there was a fight. The only wedding I could recall where the fight had been between two bridesmaids, Bonnie, and another girl.

The following morning she couldn't remember what they'd fought about. Actually, she couldn't remember the fight, but then again, she couldn't remember my name, either. I gave her my business card when I drove her home, hoping she'd call. She never did.

"Bonnie Lowry," I said and watched as she strutted toward one of my client chairs.

"Yeah, baby, told you I'd call."

"I just didn't think it would take you ten years."

"You could have called me, the phone works both ways," she said.

"I'd need your number to do that. Remember, that was one of the things you were going to call me about, your phone number."

"Oh, yeah, I suppose. I guess I took a little detour. I got married to a guy for a while, divorced the deadbeat. Got three kids, now."

"Really. Congratulations."

"Yeah, they're pretty good on most days."

"So, what brings you around?"

She glanced at the binoculars I'd set on the desk, then looked over my shoulder and out the window. "I see you're still *investigating*."

"I'm into bird watching."

"Yeah, sure you are. Mind if I sit down?"

"Oh, please, please. You want some coffee?"

"Yeah, I guess I'd take a mug, black. I mean, if you're having some."

The coffee pot was on top of the file cabinet. Fortunately, my officemate, Louie, had left his mug next to the pot. Maybe a half-inch of yesterday's coffee sat in the mug. I stepped into the closet, poured the coffee into the sink, and refilled Louie's mug.

The entire process couldn't have taken more than twenty seconds. By the time I set the mug in front of her,

Bonnie was looking across the street through the binoculars. "I see you're watching large-breasted chickadees," she said, then shook her head and set the binoculars down. She gave me a look as if to say, '*It figures,*' then took a sip of coffee. She grimaced and pushed the mug as far away from her as possible.

"So what can I do for you?"

"I'm not sure, and maybe there's nothing you can do. But I have to try something. I've got a small business."

"Oh?"

"Yeah, started out on the kitchen table a couple of years back, actually one of the many reasons for my divorce. I should back up. I took a bunch of night classes on computers and the internet and then I started going freelance, you know building a website for one business, helping someone else market products, helping another company build a customer base. Anyway, I'm into online action."

"Online action? You putting selfies out there?" I joked.

Suddenly a serious look spread across her face. "I only did that once. Well, okay, maybe a couple of times, but I'll be the first to admit it wasn't my brightest idea. I think there were some beverages involved. How did you see them?"

"Actually, I was just joking, Bonnie."

"Oh, yeah, I ahh, I knew that. Anyway, here's the deal. The people I work with, my clients, are all competing in one way or another with Amazon. So, I've been working to give them, my clients, a higher profile and then, theoretically, more business. It takes a lot of time, and at the end of the day I only have a finite amount of time. Whether it's eight or sixteen hours a day, at some point, I'm limited. See what I'm saying?"

"Maybe, I'm not exactly sure how I would fit in. The last thing you want is me on your computer or marketing your customer's products. I'd drive everyone out of business."

"Actually, that doesn't really surprise me. For the past year, I've been working nights and weekends developing a software product that would make it easy for my customers to do what I'm doing for them now."

"But wait a minute, wouldn't that put you out of business?"

"It would put me out of the business I'm currently in. But I could increase my client base by thousands, millions actually, if I can get people to buy this new software package."

"Sounds great, I wouldn't really have a use for it, but I wish you all success and…"

"Let me finish. I've got a partner, Ignatius Arnold. I want you to watch him."

"Watch him? Are you afraid he's going to rip you off or…?"

"No, no, nothing like that. He's special, a very special person. What I'm trying to say is he doesn't quite relate to the real world. He's brilliant, a computer genius, as a matter of fact. But he has a lot of issues. He's very vulnerable, and I think at least one of my competitors is trying to take advantage of him."

"Is he some kind of nerd?"

"That would be putting it mildly."

Three

I followed Bonnie over to her home so I could meet this Ignatius guy.

Before we left, she told me, "You know how they say a *picture* is worth a thousand words? Well, you meet Iggy just once, and it's like getting the whole book. He's been living in my lower level for the past six months."

Bonnie lived in Woodbury, a suburb due east of St. Paul. It was an uneventful, twelve-minute drive on I-94 from my office to her place. I pulled into the driveway behind her. Her home was a split level that wasn't more than fifteen years old. It had an attached double garage and a soccer net in the front yard with three boys about nine or ten kicking a black and white ball around. What was left of the flowers in the front of the house looked like they'd fallen victim to more than one soccer match, except for about a half-dozen daisies at the far end of the front garden that had somehow managed to survive. Morton popped his head up in the backseat, checked out the kids playing with the soccer ball, and gave a little whine.

"Mom, there's nothing good to eat," the shortest of the three boys said as Bonnie got out of her car. He was blonde and looked a lot like her, including that space between his two front teeth.

"Then you'll just have to wait for dinner, J.D.," Bonnie said and headed for the front door, I had to hurry to catch up. "This is my friend Mr. Haskell. He's going to be helping Iggy and me."

"Hi," J.D. said, then focused on lining up his next kick, ignoring me completely. He gave the ball a boot, and it sailed over the net and out into the street.

"Come on in and ignore the mess," she said, walking into the house. I followed.

The entryway was maybe eight by ten feet and covered with black and white tile, I think. There were a half-dozen Barbie dolls, an odd assortment of shoes, two nerf guns, a bucket full of legos, a blue windbreaker, what looked like a broken bicycle lock, and a toy truck scattered around the entry. A short staircase led up to the main floor, and a carpeted staircase led down to the closed door on the lower level.

Bonnie headed up the stairs to the main floor, and I dutifully followed.

"I'll give him a call and let him know we're coming. You want anything? A coffee? A beer? I think there's a couple of Cokes left in the fridge. Go ahead and just help yourself. I'm running to the bathroom."

"I'm fine, don't hurry on my account."

The living room was large, with a peaked ceiling. The room morphed into a kitchen in one corner separated by a counter of beige granite. Cereal dishes and milk glasses were stacked in the sink. A half-filled coffee mug from Las Vegas with lipstick along the edge sat on the end of the kitchen counter.

On the far side of the counter was a dining room table with eight chairs around it and a sticker book featuring whatever the latest Disney movie was. The characters looked familiar, but I was way too out of touch to even guess at the names. At the far end of the dining room table was a sliding door that led out to a fairly large deck. The living room area featured a glass-topped coffee table in front of a chocolate brown 'L' shaped couch. A large flatscreen TV sat on top of a cabinet opposite the couch. A kid's blanket was balled up on the coffee table with three toy trucks parked beneath.

I examined the dozen or so framed photos on the wall. Bonnie, with the three kids, two boys, and a girl. The boy I'd seen playing soccer in the front yard looked to be the oldest. Based on the photos, I guessed the kids might be two years apart. I was examining a picture of Bonnie and the kids at a beach somewhere, clearly not Minnesota. Given the age of her oldest, I think she called him J.D., the photo might have been taken two years ago. After three kids, she still cut a stunning figure in a bikini, although it looked like she'd added a half dozen more tattoos over the years.

"Ignore that photo, I look fat," she said, stepping out of the bathroom.

"You kidding? You look great. I'm guessing this was a couple of years ago?"

"Yeah, Nags Head, really gorgeous. It was shortly after the divorce, and we all needed to get away. It turned out to be just what the doctor ordered, sun, surf, and acting stupid. On the drive home, when we weren't singing Bingo or Old MacDonald Had a Farm, I came up with the idea of a simple link, just one click, to handle everyone's marketing needs. We got back here, and the rest is history. Let me give Iggy a call. He always likes a heads up before I knock on the door. Otherwise, he probably won't answer."

I returned to studying the photos. Bonnie pushed a speed-dial button and started speaking a moment later.

"Yeah, Iggy. Hi, it's Bonnie. No, not a problem. I was thinking pasta, with chicken tonight, interested? No, I know. Okay, hot dogs it is. No, probably not until 5:30. Listen, I've got my friend, Dev Haskell, here. Yeah. No, I don't think so. No, I understand, we'll see you in fifteen minutes. Sure, thanks."

I turned from the photos on the wall. "Everything okay?"

"Yeah, he's just in the middle of something, and he needs some time to get ready."

"Get ready?"

"I think you'll understand once you meet him."

I nodded and turned back to the photos on the wall. "So this is J.D., what's that stand for?"

"Jack Daniels. Actually, it was after that wedding of my sister, Chrissy."

"Your sister?"

"Yeah. I married one of the groomsmen, Wayne. I don't know if you met him that day. I'd been seeing him and, well, we were married about seven months later."

I could have mentioned that she'd spent the night of her sister's wedding with me, but why? "Okay, so Jack Daniels, then you had your daughter," I said, pointing at the little girl in the beach photo.

"Yeah, my sweetie, Stella. And before you ask, yes, she was named after Stella Atrois, the beer. And the baby there, he's the youngest, Bud."

"After Budweiser?" I joked.

"Exactly," she said, not kidding. "The two youngest are at daycare right now. I pick them up around four. You sure you don't want a coffee or something? I'm going to make a fresh pot. We've got a few minutes before we go downstairs."

"Yeah, okay, I'll have some coffee. So, I can't be the first person to ask about the kid's names."

She set the timer on the oven, then pulled the coffee pot out and poured the remnants of the pot into the sink. She filled the pot with water and poured it into the coffee maker. She opened a cabinet and pulled out a coffee filter, placed it in the coffee maker, then pushed a button on a grinder that whirled and ground coffee beans.

Finally she said, "Well, J.D. was a natural, because of the theme at my sister's wedding…"

Once again, I remembered we, she and I, had enjoyed a one-night stand the night of her sister's wedding, but I didn't mention it.

"…Stella seemed like a natural, and she likes it because she's the only Stella in her class. Once we had the first two named, Buddy seemed like a natural. He's a laid back little guy, exactly the type of kid you'd probably call Buddy, anyway. So, we just stayed with the theme and named him Budweiser."

Four

We chatted for a few minutes drinking coffee until the timer on the oven went off with a ding. "Okay," she said, took a sip, then set her mug on the counter. "Let's go introduce you to Iggy." I followed her down the steps toward the front door, then down the carpeted set of steps to the lower level where she knocked on the closed door.

A moment later, a muffled voice from the other side asked, "Who's there?"

Bonnie looked back at me, rolled her eyes, and said, "It's me, Iggy, and Mr. Haskell, the security specialist."

"Just the two of you?"

"Yes."

A lock snapped, and then the door opened. The room was fairly dark, illuminated by a number of computer screens giving off a blueish aura to the areas around them. I counted at least ten screens, all with bits of data and lines of code running across them.

"How's it going?" Bonnie asked, walking into the darkened room.

"Making progress," a voice said from somewhere in the dark, then closed the door behind me.

"Iggy, this is my friend Dev Haskell. We go back a long way. He's the private investigator I told you about."

"Could I see some identification?" a squeaky voice asked.

I waited half a moment for the laugh, signifying a joke, but it didn't happen. "Yeah, sure, will a driver's license do? I've got my VA card, a five-dollar gift card to Target, a…"

"Just the driver's license, please."

I handed him my license. He clicked on a small flashlight, examined the license, flashed the light in my face, and studied me for a moment, then handed the license back to me. "Thank you."

I attempted to regain my vision as he walked toward a bank of computer screens. I could just make out a tall, thin figure who could have been the poster child for the nerd club. He wore glasses in black frames, the kind of frames kids in grade school wore, with very thick lenses. He had an exceptionally high forehead with hair of medium length sticking out at various angles. The hair was anything but trendy, rather more like an eternal bedhead. He wore a Star Wars t-shirt, Luke Skywalker with a lightsaber, with the words 'The Force Awakens' below the image, and a pair of suspenders. I guessed the silver sheet he had wrapped around his shoulders was most likely Mylar. The cap he wore appeared to be tinfoil. I extended my hand, wondering if he'd shake it. He did, although I noted he wore latex gloves and was in desperate need of a shower.

"Bonnie told me you develop software," I said, trying to ignore the weirdness in front of me.

"Yes, yes, I can give you a little demonstration, if you'd like."

"Please, I'd like that," I lied.

"Come over here," he said and hurried toward a bank of three computer screens. At this point, Bonnie was drifting off in the darkness somewhere. Iggy sat down in front of the three screens and indicated a chair next to him. As I sat, I noticed a number of what looked like Star Wars figures scattered around the desk. I could make out a couple of posters on the wall, Star Wars again, I think, but it was too dark in the far recesses of the room to be sure.

"So what we need to do is offer a multi-lingual methodology to our clients with just the touch of a button." He went on from there, rapidly clicking the keyboard as he spoke, although that opening line was about the only thing I understood. It was clear he was in his element, constantly going off on a tangent, maybe mentioning the occasional something to Bonnie, who seemed to understand what was being said. From my point of view, they might as well have been speaking Latin. Fortunately, it was dark enough in the room that neither one could pick up the blank look on my face. After about twenty minutes, there was a pause in the conversation, and Iggy's hands came off the keyboard.

"Very interesting. So, tell me how you envision using my services?" I said.

Iggy gave a slight shrug, rubbed his latex-gloved hands back and forth, and stared into the dark beneath the desk.

"We're about to bring the product online. I can go over funding with you in a bit, suffice to say it's no longer the best kept secret, and we've had, umm, some unwanted interest," Bonnie said.

"There's been a substantial increase in the electromagnetic field," Iggy added, raising his eyes upward toward his tinfoil hat. "Scanning my brain, most likely attempting to read the code, possibly an effort at mind control, mind reading. It's been increasing steadily for the past six months. I thought things would improve when I moved in here, but they found me. I can't imagine what would happen if I ventured outside."

I nodded like I understood, then looked into the dark where I thought Bonnie was standing. Her voice suddenly sounded about ten feet to the left of where I thought she would be. "Well, as you can see, Iggy, we've got a top-notch private investigator, a real security specialist, on the case so you won't have to worry about it anymore."

"Do you have a relationship with the highway department?" Iggy asked.

"The highway department?"

"Yeah," Bonnie inserted herself. "Iggy's been aware of the efforts of the highway department to read his mind for quite some time. If I recall correctly, you stated in your interview that you had no relationship with them. You do not work for them, and you never have worked for them."

"Yeah, that's right." I nodded, then swiveled my chair to face Iggy and embellished. "I have absolutely no relationship with the highway department, never have, never will." This seemed to bring a smile to his face, and he flashed a mouthful of crooked teeth, suggesting I'd passed the test.

"We'll let you get back to work, Iggy. I just wanted you to meet Dev, so if you see him around, he's just here to help and to keep everyone safe, especially you."

"It was a pleasure to meet you, Mr. Haskell," Iggy said and giggled in a certifiable way.

"The pleasure was all mine, Iggy. Keep up the good work."

"Come on, Dev, I'll show you our files," Bonnie said and suddenly stepped out of the dark.

Iggy followed us to the door, making a weird giggling noise along the way. The moment we stepped out, he closed the door, and then a lock snapped shut.

"You gotta be kidding me," I half-whispered.

"Shhh," Bonnie put a finger to her lips, then pointed upstairs to the main floor.

Five

Bonnie opened up a cabinet and took out two glasses, then held them under the ice dispenser on the refrigerator door until they were filled with ice. "Well, what do you think?" she half-whispered up in the kitchen.

"Just a Coke for me, Bonnie. What do I think? My first question would be, are you guys safe? No offense, but he's not exactly playing on a level field."

"But he's a genius. The software he's written is flawless. All the work he's done would have taken a team an entire year, and he's done it all, on his own, in half the time."

"Does he ever sleep? I don't mean to sound rude, but I'm not sure where to even begin."

"Well, yes, he does sleep, maybe. As near as I can figure out, he seems to be on lunar schedule."

"What in the hell is a lunar schedule?"

"You know, the lunar calendar. He basically does his best work when the moon is full."

"Are you kidding? What the hell does he do when there's a lunar eclipse or clouds?"

"That can be problematic."

"Bonnie, maybe you've heard this once or twice before, but that guy really needs some professional help and a lot of it."

"But he's a genius, Dev. I'm not kidding, the programs he's written, we're going to take the market by storm."

"Just for the sake of argument, let's say you do. You think your pal downstairs is going to be able to handle that? I mean, for starters, he might have to be exposed to daylight. God forbid he'd take a shower."

"Very funny. That's my job, handling sales, doing the marketing. I'll do a couple of presentations for Google, Amazon, maybe Facebook, or even Twitter and offer them an exclusive contract, first come first served. Once the bidding starts, I expect to be on easy street within the next six weeks. Just in case that doesn't work, I can offer the product to individuals."

"So, what do you want me to do?"

"Do? I don't expect you to do anything, really. Other than make Iggy feel safe. He's got some fine-tuning to do on his programs, and, as you may have picked up, he's got a bit of a tendency to obsess."

"So there really isn't a threat? No one is trying to steal his secrets? No one is attempting to steal his programs? No one's trying to read his mind?"

"I just said that stuff to make him feel, umm, not so alone."

"Not feel alone? The guy is wrapped in tin foil!"

"It's Mylar, actually."

"Well, there you go. What about the kids?"

She flashed a quick smile. "They're leaving in two days to spend a month at my sister's lake place over in Wisconsin. I expect to have everything signed, sealed and delivered by the time they're back."

"Doesn't sound like you're leaving yourself very much time."

"Honey, once they see our demonstration, it'll just become a bidding war, and the highest bidder wins. It's simple."

I figured I had to be missing something. "So, I'm still not clear what it is you want me to do."

"Well, make it look to Iggy like you're providing security. I expect I'll be doing some traveling. Maybe you could make sure he's comfortable."

"Comfortable?"

"Yeah, while I'm gone, you know."

"It sounds like you want me to babysit."

"That might be too strong a term. I can promise you there'll be some additional *benefits* thrown in along with a paycheck."

"Would it be okay if I called you tomorrow? I'm guessing you'd like me to start after your kids leave for the lake."

"Okay, but call me before noon because if you can't do it, I'm going to have to find somebody else."

"Fair enough. Nice to see you again, Bonnie."

"Told you I'd be in touch," she said.

'Ten years ago,' I thought but didn't mention that piece of information. "Yeah, you did. Okay, I'll give you a call tomorrow."

"Hope you say yes," she said, then raised her eyebrows and ran her tongue over her upper lip.

"I better get going," I said and headed down the stairs and out the front door. One of the kids, probably J.D., had let Morton out of the car, and the three boys were tossing a nuclear pink frisbee to him. All that remained of the daisies at the far end of the front garden was some petals scattered across the lawn, victims of the frisbee, Morton, or a combination of the two.

"Come on, Morton, let's go, buddy." Morton ran to the car with the frisbee and hopped in the backseat as I held the door for him. I wrestled the frisbee out of his mouth, and he turned his attention to the rawhide he'd been chewing earlier.

I flicked the frisbee to J.D., who said, "Can Morton come back?"

"Yeah, it looks like he had a pretty good time. I'll bring him back. Thanks for playing with him."

"He was really fun," one of the other kids said.

Morton was asleep in the backseat two blocks later.

Six

L ouie asked, "And you're sure she's going to pay you?"

"Yeah, plus *benefits*," I said, raising my eyebrows.

We'd stopped for one in The Spot bar about two hours ago. AC/DC's 'It's a Long Way to the Top (If You Wanna Rock 'n' Roll)' was playing for the third time in a row on the jukebox and two over-served young women were dancing at the end of the bar. We ignored them, but Morton was paying attention. He was at my feet, eating from a bag of pork rinds one of the girls had bought him, watching them dance.

"I don't know, man, it sounds kind of screwy."

"Of course it's screwy. But this guy has been living in the dark in her lower level for the last half-year working on his computers twenty-four hours a day, seven days a week. All I have to do is keep the highway department away so they can't read his mind. I think I can handle it. Plus, since Angie suddenly got all responsible and started thinking about the future instead of my immediate gratification, I've been heading toward a bit of a dry spell. Bonnie would be a welcome relief from that circumstance.”

Louie drained his drink, threw another twenty on the bar, and slid off the stool, shaking his head. “I don’t know, man, it just doesn’t sound right. Hey, I’ll see you guys in the morning,” he said and gave Morton a rub behind the ear, then walked out the door.

I had another beer, watched the girls dancing to the jukebox, it was still AC/DC, still the same song. They were dancing around in circles with their hands above their heads, shouting, “Whoo, hoo, hoo.” They continued to grind off each other’s hips and wave their hands over their heads until, finally, even I couldn’t stand it anymore.

“Come on, Morton, let’s go home,” I said and slid off the stool. Morton hurried to the door, I think more anxious to get out of there than me. “Thanks, Jimmy.”

“Take me with you,” he half pleaded. He was leaning on the bar, resting his chin in his hand, watching the girls dance. “I’m gonna delete that song as soon as they leave.”

“Maybe they won’t leave, they’ll just stay here forever. You could offer drinks and dancing and…”

“Don’t even go there.”

* * *

We were in the office the following morning. Morton was napping on the floor, and I was scanning the apartment across the street, looking for some cheap shots. There weren't any. Louie wandered in around half-past nine, threw a computer bag on his picnic table desk, then wandered toward the coffee pot. He grabbed his mug and dumped the remnants down the sink in the closet. "Is this from yesterday?" he asked, filling his mug.

"No, I made it fresh this morning."

"Oh, wow, you're kidding, great," he said, took a sip, grimaced, then headed back to the picnic table. "So, you come up with a decision?"

"You mean Bonnie? Yeah, I don't think I can go two more days in this dry spell, so I'm going to ask her over for dinner tonight, and hopefully, we can consummate the deal before she goes home."

Louie stared at me for a moment, then shook his head and sat down. "So, you're going to do it with her?"

"Yeah. I mean, I get it, she's kind of screwy, but she's basically nice and has a great body, so…"

"I meant the deal, security, or babysitting or what-ever you're supposed to do."

"Are you kidding, why wouldn't I? I'll occasionally walk around the exterior of the house. Maybe pull up a lawn chair out on that back deck and work on my tan for an hour or two. Have a cold one toward the end of the day, and I'll be getting paid for it the whole time. Not to mention taking care of Bonnie's needs. Does the term 'cake walk' have any connotation?"

Louie just shook his head. "Something's bound to go wrong."

"Yeah, I suppose the highway department could scan all the information out of Iggy's brain. Or they could read my mind…

"That would be an awfully short story."

"Very funny. I've got it covered. I think I'll go over there with a couple rolls of tinfoil, make sure the lower level windows are covered. It was too dark, but I'm guessing there was a sliding door leading out to the backyard. I'll put some foil over that if Iggy hasn't done so already, just to get him calmed down and relaxed. Make sure the highway department doesn't break in and try and carry him off. I'm telling you, this is gonna be one of the better gigs of the year - no, the last five years."

"Sure, just like the time you were going to pull security in the shower room for all the girls on that English Roller Derby team."

"Well, yeah, but that chick was nuts."

"And a guy wrapped in tinfoil isn't?"

Seven

I phoned Bonnie later that morning and told her I'd like to discuss things further. "I'm wondering if you might be available for dinner tonight, I was thinking I'd cook steaks on the grill."

"Tonight? Yeah, I think I can do that, in fact, I'll bring dessert," she said and gave an evil laugh.

Bonnie arrived at seven. We'd just returned from Morton's walk. I wanted to make sure he was well exercised and hopefully, on the tired side before Bonnie and I sat down to dinner. I'd just given him a new rawhide, and he'd curled up in his bed in front of the living room couch.

She was wearing a pink tube top that barely contained her attributes. Extremely tight white shorts that extended no further than the very top of her thighs and then high heeled white boots that rose up to about six inches above her knee, therefore exposing the upper six inches of perfect skin on her thighs. She looked awfully sexy. The horn-honking and the whistle from some guy driving past as she climbed out of the car caught my attention. I watched her strut across the sidewalk, then up the steps to my front porch.

A couple was walking past, and the guy stared to the point where he was looking over his shoulder before his wife yanked his hand and said something to him. I couldn't hear what she said, but the body language was unmistakable. He just shrugged, and they kept on going.

I opened the door a half-second after the doorbell rang. "Hey, Bonnie, you found the place okay?"

"Yeah, I was here once before, I think, wasn't I?" So much for memorable occasions.

"Gee, you look great, come on in."

"Oh, hey, you redid the place," she said, stepping in.

"Actually, no, it's the same as when you were last here." I didn't add she was last here ten years ago.

"Hmmm, could have fooled me. Whoa, and who's this?" She asked as Morton gave his usual greeting, thrusting his nose up between her legs.

"Oh, yeah, sorry. That's Morton, my dog, I guess. He was playing frisbee with the kids in your front yard." Morton's tail was wagging back and forth, and at least for the moment, Bonnie seemed a better option than his new rawhide.

"Oh, he's so sweet. What did you mean, you guess he's yours? Did you rescue him?"

"Long story, he saved my life. The woman who had him moved to Atlanta and the guy she's with apparently had an allergy, so I got Morton."

"He saved your life?"

"Yeah, literally, I was working a case, a big dog show. Anyway, he's a pretty good boy." Morton was still in the greeting mode, and I had to pull him away. "Come on, pal, back to your treat, go on into your bed."

"Oh, I really don't mind, I think he's cute."

"Not to worry, once we bring the steaks in off the grill, he'll be right there. Come on back to the kitchen," I said and led the way.

We were out on the deck. Bonnie was sipping a glass of wine. I had a beer going. Potatoes, red peppers, and the steaks were all on the grill, and we'd been chatting about what exactly I was supposed to do.

"Like I said yesterday, a big part of it is just making Iggy feel comfortable. Just in case you didn't pick up on it, he has a tendency to obsess."

"A tendency? The guy is wrapped in tinfoil and…"

"Actually, it's Mylar."

"…and he thinks the highway department is trying to read his mind. You said he's a genius, and he's written all these programs for you."

"Yeah. To be honest, he's really sweet. There might be a couple of things that are, umm, maybe a little unusual…"

"There's an understatement."

"Well, I think a lot of it stems from when he was working for the government. He did all sorts of things in—"

"The government. What? Don't tell me he was actually working on programs to read minds?"

"No," she said and took a sip of wine. "At least not that I know of. I do know that he was in Iraq and Afghanistan, a couple other places, Syria, for sure, and somewhere in Africa."

"What department did he work for?" This sounded kind of crazy.

"The department, I don't know. Something with all sorts of letters, you know, one of those acronyms, he told me once, but it didn't make any sense to me."

"How'd you ever find him?"

"We met online. No," she said in response to my look. "Not a dating site. I was on a number of different sites asking questions regarding the software I was trying to develop, and he kept giving me these great suggestions and answers. Then, when I found out he was actually living in the area, after about three dozen emails back and forth, I was able to set up a meeting."

"He agreed to meet you? Amazing, considering he had to see my driver's license even with you making the introduction."

"Well, let me tell you, I had to send him something like a resume. He wanted to know where I'd been living the past fifteen years, places of employment, education, Facebook sites, email addresses."

"And you agreed to give him all that?"

"You bet. Dev, like I told you yesterday, the guy has developed the program in easily half the time it would have taken a team to do the work, and I would have had to pay them."

"You're not paying him?"

"No. I mean he gets to live there for free, I buy the groceries, pay the bills."

"But still he has to have some need for funds, I don't know maybe insurance? A car? God forbid he'd ever want to go out and see a movie."

"To tell you the truth, he hasn't ventured outside since the day he moved into the lower level. He doesn't own a car. I don't know about insurance, I've never asked."

"So day in and day out he's just been working on this program he's developed?"

"Yeah, I mean, I know it sounds crazy, and you're exactly right. When I finally got to meet him, I went to his place. It was this hell-hole, one room, little basement apartment just off of downtown. There was graffiti written all over his door, I saw a mouse running under a chair, cobwebs, drippy faucet, it was just awful and as we talked he alluded to some of the other tenants abusing him."

"What do you mean, abusing him?"

"Well, I just told you about the graffiti. I guess they'd chase him if he went to the grocery store or if they caught him outside. He'd been robbed a number of times. I think assaulted more than once."

"Do you think he's crazy?"

"Yeah, a little, but then, aren't we all? He's a genius, he's very gentle, and he's very kind."

"As long as there's plenty of tinfoil to go around."

"Don't pick on him, Dev."

"Okay, sorry."

"Anyway, when I saw how he was living, and he told me some of the things that had happened to him, the assaults, the robberies, and here he was just trying to help me with the program I was trying to get off the ground, well, I brought him home that day, and he moved into the lower level."

"You hauled all those computers in, his furniture, and stuff?"

"We, or rather I, got some people who owed me a favor to help. It really wasn't that much. I mean, once you got past all the computer stuff. I think he sleeps on the floor in a sleeping bag. He brought a couple of desk chairs, a coffee mug, one set of silverware, and that was about it. Oh, yeah, and about four dozen Star Wars t-shirts."

"How could I forget, 'The Force Awakens'."

"Exactly," she said and drained her glass.

"Tell you what, if you want to carry your wine glass in, I'll take everything off the grill. Hope you don't mind, I figured we'd just eat at the kitchen counter."

"As long as I'm not cooking and three kids aren't turning their noses up at whatever I just made, it's wonderful."

"Come on. I'll refill your glass."

Eight

The steaks were done to perfection if I do say so myself. We had an enjoyable meal and chatted about everything and nothing. Bonnie gave me some general information about her ex. Turns out the guy more or less abandoned her and the kids, and she filed a restraining order against him about three years ago. "The only time he ever gets in contact with me is when he wants something, usually money, by the way."

"What does he think about Iggy?"

"As far as I know, he's unaware Iggy's even there. I guess that's another reason I wanted you there. If Wayne ever showed up, it would be just like him to create a scene. I know we all make mistakes, but for the life of me, I can't remember what I ever saw in him."

"Didn't you tell me you met him at your sister's wedding?"

"Yeah. He was actually doing the girl I had the disagreement with, and…"

"Disagreement? It was more like you two bridesmaids had a fistfight. If you'll recall I had to pull you off of her, you gave her a bloody nose."

"Well, no doubt she had it coming, and as far as having to pull me off of her, I thought you were just copping a feel, and I figured, hmmm, this could be interesting."

"Probably not too far from the truth."

"So the next day, remember, you gave me a ride back to the bar so I could get my purse."

"Yeah, and you ran into some friend who said he'd give you a ride home."

"Only he wasn't really a friend, that was Wayne, and I really didn't know him, well, anyway, not till later that night. Our first time together. Turned out two cheeseburgers and a bunch of shots later, I'm pregnant."

"Really, first time?"

"Well, with him. Dopey me, I figured getting pregnant was a sign from heaven that we were meant for each other. We got married a couple of months before J.D. was born."

"And that's how he got the name, Jack Daniels? Because it was the wedding theme?"

"That and the fact we were doing shots. Of course, one thing led to another, and Wayne had this big backseat and, well, anyway. Then, just about the time I was thinking of leaving him. First Stella appeared on the scene and then little Buddy. After Buddy, even I learned my lesson and, although it hasn't been easy, things have definitely been on an upward swing once I got old Wayne out of my hair," she said. She tilted her right hand at about a forty-five-degree angle to indicate the upward swing.

"And now you're about to launch this new program."

"Yeah, and I'll be the first to admit it would not be done, and in fact, might never have been accomplished if Iggy and I hadn't met. So, back to your point, is he crazy? I suppose yeah, in a variety of different ways. He's definitely got some quirky little habits. But, at the end of the day, I'd be nowhere near where I am if it weren't for Iggy, and I'll always want to make sure he's safe and happy."

"You really think this program is going to do what you hope?"

"Absolutely. It's just a matter of getting it in front of people so they can see for themselves, and then we can sit back and watch who makes the best offer."

"You ready for some dessert?" I had some Snickers ice cream bars in the freezer.

"I told you, I'd take care of that."

"Oh, sorry, I didn't notice you bringing anything in."

She smiled, hopped off the kitchen stool, then ran her hands from her shoulders down to her waist and stood there with her arms outstretched. "Help yourself."

I figured the dishes could wait.

* * *

She woke me with a kiss, already dressed. "No, you don't have to get up, stay in bed. I have to go. My sitter has to be home by one. I'll let myself out."

I rolled out of bed, got a nice long kiss and a passionate grab.

"Oh, God, now I want to stay," she said. "But I have to go. Stop by tomorrow, and I'll show you around, the kids are on their way to the lake around one, so anytime after that works."

I pulled on a t-shirt and followed her downstairs. "Thanks for a memorable evening," she said at the door, then gave me a quick kiss and was gone.

Morton was asleep in his bed. I stared for a moment at the remnants of a white silk thong, Bonnie's, that Morton had apparently chewed up and left on the floor next to his bed. I really couldn't blame him.

I went into the kitchen, cleaned up the dishes, put away the leftovers, and then headed back upstairs to bed.

Nine

I drove over to Bonnie's a little after four. I figured by the time we covered whatever she wanted to talk about, it would be close to five, and maybe I could scam a dinner from her. I brought a bottle of wine just to increase my chances. Morton was pacing in the backseat, looking for his Frisbee pals as we pulled into the drive-way. We climbed out and rang the doorbell. There seemed to be an additional sense of calm about the place with the kids gone.

Bonnie answered a minute or two later. As she opened the door, she brushed her forehead with the back of her hand. She wore a t-shirt and jeans, held a sponge in one hand, and reeked of Pine-Sol or some other clean-ing compound.

"Oh, God, Dev. I completely forgot. Chrissy picked up the kids, and I've been cleaning ever since. Nothing like two little boys with a bad aim in the bathroom."

"Keep working if you want. I can come back tomor-row."

"No, no, but I need to finish the project I'm on. Damn it, then I'll have to figure what I'm going to do for dinner. You want to come in and watch TV or something?"

"I got a better idea, why don't I get dinner, one less thing you'll have to fool with. Just take your time. If you're still cleaning when I get back, don't worry about it."

"You're sure?"

"Yeah, not a problem. Do I need to pick something up for Iggy?"

"Would you mind?"

"No, but I'm just guessing there might be a couple of things he doesn't eat. Is he a vegan, or he only eats roasted cashews or something?"

"Actually, he does have a couple of restrictions. Nothing with honey, it…"

"Honey?"

"Yeah, commercial honey enslaves bees, and when you think about it, he's kinda right."

"Okay," I said, thinking here we go.

"And if you're planning on getting any kind of fruit, just make sure it isn't something that would harm the plant if it's picked."

"Is there something he likes? Maybe it would just be easier to go that route."

"Hot dogs, he eats a lot of hot dogs, an awful lot."

"Okay, I'll get him hot dogs. You and I will dine on something a little more elegant."

"Is this too much of a pain?"

"No, it's not, and if I'm going to be covering for you while you're gone a day or two, I should probably know this stuff anyway. You hungry for anything special?"

"Just something I don't have to cook."

"I'll be back within the hour. Take your time. If you want to keep working, go ahead. I'll just watch." She was wearing some kind of stretch jeans and appeared to have no bra on beneath her t-shirt. I could only hope she'd be scrubbing floors when I returned.

I stopped at a Thai restaurant and got two orders of chicken fried rice to go, plus a starter of chicken on skewers with a satay sauce. I had them toss in an extra container of satay sauce just because I like it. Then I went to the grocery store and picked up a package of hot dogs and a bag of buns for Iggy. God, I felt like I was shopping for a ten-year-old.

I was back in an hour on the dot. Bonnie had left a note on the door. "Dev, I'm in the shower, come on in."

I presumed she meant, come on into the house, not necessarily the shower. I set the bag on the kitchen counter, set the counter for two, then proceeded to boil hot dogs for Iggy and Morton. When the hot dogs were ready, I placed Iggy's on two buns, draped the plate with Saran Wrap, and carried it down to the lower level.

I knocked loudly on his door. After some time, a muffled voice, sounding a little frightened, asked, "Who, who is it?"

"Hi, Iggy. It's Dev Haskell, the security specialist. Bonnie's in the shower, and she suggested I cook up some dinner. I've got a couple of hot dogs for you."

"Just just leave them out there by the door."

"Yeah, okay, no problem. I'll set them on the stairs, here," I said, doing exactly that. "Great talking to you, Iggy. Enjoy. Hey, do you need mustard or catsup?"

"I have my own down here, thank you."

"Okay, catch you later." I hurried to the upper level, then leaned over the open stairwell and waited. A few minutes later, I heard the lock unsnap, and the door slowly opened. Iggy took a cautious step outside his room. I could hear the Mylar sheet rustling before I saw him. He had more tinfoil wrapped around his head and wore another pair of latex gloves. He bent down and waved some black device over the food like he was holding a metal detector or checking for radiation. Apparently satisfied, he picked up the plate, hurried back into his room, then snapped the lock the moment he closed the door.

"What exactly are you doing?" Bonnie asked from behind.

"I just delivered two hot dogs downstairs, and I wanted to see what he would do."

"And?"

"I guess it went okay, at least it seemed to. He waved a box or something over them, then brought them back into his lair."

"That was the detector he waved over them."

"The detector. And what, exactly, is it supposed to detect?"

"It changes depending on the day, some days toxic fumes, other days electromagnetic rays, although I've never had him turn anything down. So, if he's eating hot dogs, what did you get for us?"

"I hope you like Thai. I picked up chicken fried rice and some chicken with satay sauce."

"Perfect. It's a gorgeous evening, mind if we eat out on the deck?"

"I'd love it."

"You in any hurry?"

"No, not really."

"Why don't we start with a glass of wine. I feel like I've been going a mile a minute ever since the kids left."

"If you have a beer, I'd take that, more wine for you."

"I'll get the glasses if you'll grab the wine out of the fridge. There are a couple of whites in there. I think one might already be open. The beer is on the bottom shelf in the back."

We sat out on the deck, enjoying the evening. The picnic table looked home-made, and we sat in a couple of aluminum lawn chairs. I actually had two beers. Bonnie finished what had been left of the open bottle of wine. We were just chatting after dinner, largely gossip, when out of the blue, she said, "I suppose I should tell you. I think I saw Wayne today."

"Wayne, your ex? That Wayne?"

"Yeah, it was just as we were loading the kids in the car. Fortunately, they didn't see him, although J.D. is the only one who might recognize him, and I'm not even sure about that."

"Maybe he just happened to drive past."

Bonnie looked at me like I was nuts. "This is one of those streets where you're either lost, or you're going to visit someone who lives here. He wasn't lost."

"So, you think he was coming to see you?"

"That would be the worst scenario. The best would be he was checking the place out before he came to see me. Not much better than the first scenario. On the other hand, my sister, Chrissy, was here, and the two of them have never gotten along."

"So I should probably keep an eye out. What does he drive?"

"A shiny, red, F-150 pickup truck with flames painted on the hood. Real hard to miss."

"And you're sure it was him?"

"Yeah, idiot tried to duck down as he drove past, then he floored it going down the street just in case I didn't notice."

"Any idea what he might want?"

"No. Whatever it is, he's not getting any. I'm reasonably sure he's up to no good."

"When was the last time you saw him?"

"About forty-eight hours after I filed the restraining order. Right after Buddy was born, so call it three years ago."

"Strange, he'd turn up now."

"Not really, he always had a knack for ruining whatever wonderful event was about to happen. God only knows what I ever saw in him. Hey, how about some dinner?"

Ten

We'd been asleep for a while. According to the digital clock on Bonnie's dresser, it was almost four in the morning. She had a smile on her face and was breathing heavily, not quite a soft snore but almost. God knows she'd earned it. I studied her for a long moment. She'd left the bathroom light on and closed the door, but the sliver of light escaping was just enough to let me see her clearly. In the past ten years, she'd added a star tattoo around her pierced navel, and then below that, a red ribbon that wrapped all the way around her waist and ended up in a big red bow between her thighs. It gave one the impression you were about to open up a gift, which actually wasn't too far from the truth.

I heard something bump outside the bedroom, and my first thought was Morton, but then he poked me in the back with his cold nose and whined. The noise seemed to be coming from out in the kitchen. I rolled out of bed and pulled on my boxers, thinking maybe Iggy was up raiding the refrigerator. I opened the bedroom door, the house was dark, which probably made Iggy feel right at home. I heard the noise again and quietly made my way down the hall. Morton hung back in the bed-room. I cautiously peeked around the corner into the kitchen area, but couldn't see anything.

I waited for a bit and was about to head back to bed when I heard the noise again. It was coming from out on the deck, a clicking or something. I made my way toward the sliding door. I remembered Bonnie locking it before we went to bed, and then she'd placed a board just be-hind the door so it wouldn't be able to slide open. Even if the door was left unlocked, no one would get in with the board lying there.

I heard the noise again just as I saw the shadow in the moonlight. It was actually a figure, a guy, leaning down and fiddling with the lock, I think. If he was trying to pick it he wasn't doing a very good job. As my eyes adjusted, I began to make out his features, long, thinning hair, and a large tattoo across his neck. He wore cutoff blue jeans and a t-shirt that simply said 'Grunge,' which somehow seemed to fit. It looked like he was wearing sandals.

I slowly made my way over to the far wall, then got down on all fours and crawled behind the dining room table toward the door. I picked up the board Bonnie had placed behind the sliding door. It was a 2x2, maybe three feet long. The guy was focused on the lock with his back halfway facing me. I slowly pulled the board toward me, then backtracked a foot or two until I was hidden again by the dining room table. I exhaled, then took a deep breath, stood, took three quick steps to the door, and flicked the lock, making a loud click.

Just as I pulled the door open, 'Grunge,' said, "Finally." Then he looked up, and his eyes grew wide as I slammed the 2x2 down onto his forehead like I was splitting a piece of wood. He crumpled backward onto the deck and remained very still. I unbuckled his belt, dragged him over to the deck railing, then wrapped the belt around his ankles and attached it to the railing. At this point, he was starting to groan but wasn't really moving. If he was able to sit up, and that was a big 'if' based on the massive egg growing on his forehead, he'd be here for at least a couple of minutes. I stepped back inside, pulled the door closed, locked it, then wandered back to Bonnie's bedroom. She was still sound asleep and hadn't moved. Morton had climbed into the bed and stretched out on my side.

I gently shook her shoulder, "Bonnie, wake up. Bonnie."

She rolled over on her back, said, "Hop on," and pulled the pillow over her head.

I lifted the pillow and said, "You've got a visitor. I think it might be your ex, Wayne."

Her eyes opened wide, and she focused on me. "What?"

"Some idiot was out on the deck, attempting to pick the lock on your sliding door and not doing a very good job at it."

"Did he run away? Where did he go?"

"He's, ahh, still out there. At least he was a minute ago. Maybe put something on, and you can check him out. I didn't know if you wanted to call the police."

"If it's Wayne, I want to push him off the deck," she growled and rolled out of bed. I pulled on my jeans and a t-shirt. Morton lifted his head for a moment, then went back to sleep.

Eleven

She turned on the hall light as she stepped out of the bedroom. At the end of the hall, she turned on the kitchen light and then the light out on the deck above the sliding door. Wayne, or whoever he was, held his head in his hands and was still on his back with his feet tied to the deck railing.

"Oh, Jesus Christ," Bonnie growled as she ripped the sliding door open. "Wayne, you absolute moron. What in the hell are you doing here?"

Wayne groaned a couple of times, then said, "I was just gonna stop by and maybe grab a beer?" His tone suggested he knew exactly how lame his excuse sounded, but it was the only one he could come up with.

" A beer? At four in the damn morning? You worthless piece of shit. You're three years behind on child support payments, and you think you can just sneak in here in the middle of the night and have a beer? God, you are so unbelievably stupid. And what's with your forehead? It looks like you're trying to grow something," she said, then looked at me.

I just shrugged and said, "He was trying to pick the lock, and I thought maybe that wasn't the best idea."

"Breaking into my house?" she yelled, then kicked him in the side. "I ought to call the cops on you, you stupid idiot. Now, get the hell up, come on, quit lying there like the worthless piece of shit you are and stand up."

Wayne attempted to half move his feet, then groaned, "I can't."

Bonnie looked up at me, "Dev, would you please undo that, so asshole here can get up?"

I unwrapped the belt from the railing and his ankles, then let his feet drop.

Wayne groaned but didn't do anything beyond that.

"Get up, scumbag," Bonnie half-shouted and kicked Wayne in the side again.

"God, will you please take it easy," he said and slowly began to stand. "Just in case you haven't noticed, I'm injured here. I ought to sue the both of you. What do you think about that? Think you're some kind of tough guy, blindsiding me like that, buddy? See how you like it when—"

I hit him hard. Gave Wayne a haymaker just as he was getting to his feet. I caught him on the bridge of his nose, I think I heard a 'crack' sound, but I couldn't be sure. I was pretty sure I felt his nose give way as he crumpled back onto the deck, and there was suddenly an awful lot of blood.

"Oh, God, you completely worthless shit, stop bleeding on my deck. I'll never get the stain out. Dev, sit him in the chair. Mother of God, I'll get some ice," Bonnie said, then stormed into the kitchen, muttering a variety of invectives.

I grabbed Wayne by the arm and the back of his grunge t-shirt and hoisted him into one of the lawn chairs.

"Ahh, man, you didn't have to do that. I just—"

"Let me advise you of your rights here, Wayne-o. You say one more stupid thing or in any way raise your voice or threaten Bonnie, and I promise I will throw you over the railing of this deck. You got it?"

He looked at me with blurry eyes that were already beginning to swell and nodded. I really hadn't paid attention to his nose before I hit him, but I was pretty sure it hadn't been in that 'C' shape, leaning over a good inch to the right. Blood ran down his chin and pooled onto his Grunge t-shirt, hiding three of the letters, so it just read 'GR E'.

"Here, put this up against your nose," Bonnie said and thrust what looked like a cloth diaper with ice cubes toward Wayne. "Then put this on that second head you're growing," she said and handed him a ziplock plastic bag with more ice cubes.

Wayne dutifully obeyed and suddenly, with an ice pack on his nose and another on his forehead, about all we could see of his face was his chin.

"Tilt your head back, Wayne. It'll help stop the bleeding. God, you big dope," Bonnie said, shaking her head. "What in the hell were you thinking?"

"Oh, God," Wayne groaned, tilting his head back. The egg on his forehead was an absolutely perfect rectangle almost two inches wide and three inches long. It was in the process of turning a definite purple color. His nose was probably going to require surgery, just to get it back to something vaguely normal, and then it might only serve a cosmetic function.

"Wayne, I asked you a question," Bonnie said. She was soft-spoken, but there was a decided edge to her voice, and it was pretty clear groaning wasn't going to get Wayne off the hook.

He groaned anyway, then shot her a sideways glance, checking to see if Bonnie was really serious.

"Well?"

"God, I can barely breathe. I should probably get my ass to a hospital."

"Okay, that sounds like a good idea. Let me help. I'm gonna call the cops. They'll be able to get you there faster than anyone else. Then, once the ER has finished, the police will lock you up, and you'll have plenty of time to think about an answer to my question. Sound like a good idea?"

"Ahh-Ahhh," Wayne groaned.

"That's it, I'm calling the cops," Bonnie said and pulled the door open.

"Okay, okay, just hold on. God, in case you didn't notice, I'm dealing with some major injuries here. I'm the innocent victim of an assault and—"

"Innocent victim? Wayne, so help me—"

"Alright, calm down. Look, all I know is some guy contacted me."

"Some guy?"

"Yeah, definitely a creepy-looking dude. Asked me about the layout of your place, said he was a contractor. Something about redoing your ceilings or something."

"Why would he talk to you? You've never even been here before. If you'll recall, the few times we had to meet, I insisted on a public place."

"Yeah, well, believe me, first and last time," he said, giving me a quick glance.

"How did he even know who you were?"

"I don't know, and I didn't bother to ask. He gave me a hundred dollar bill, said he just wanted to know what the layout of the joint was."

"And this didn't seem strange to you?"

"Strange? Hey, you listening? Who the hell cares? It was a hundred dollar bill."

"How'd he even know who you were? Where'd he find you?"

"Benny's, I'd just stopped for one and…"

"Figures, and no, you didn't just stop for one. You basically live there."

"It's an okay joint."

"Why would some contractor what to know about the layout here?"

"I just told you, to work on your ceiling. You telling me you don't know anything about this?"

"Wayne, if I knew about it, the guy could just come over and look, couldn't he?"

"Well, yeah, I suppose, now that you mention it."

"So someone gives my ex-husband-the-idiot, a hundred bucks to get the layout of my house, and you don't think it's strange?"

"Were you listening? I already told you, it was a hundred bucks, cash."

Twelve

Wayne was either really, really stupid or an incredibly talented liar. My money was on the first option. Bonnie gave him the third degree for another half hour, took a couple of cellphone pictures of him to document his attempted intrusion, and then had me help him into his truck.

She was right, it was a bright red F-150 with flames on the hood, and it was hard to miss. He'd parked a block away, and I had to walk over and retrieve the vehicle. There was a half-empty bottle of Jack Daniels on the front seat, stupid for at least two reasons. First, it was an open bottle in the vehicle, and second, it was in plain sight. I provided a third reason. Any more drinking from the thing would be a bad idea, I proceeded to add my own special blend until it was two-thirds full, then squirted the rest on the passenger side of the floor. I figured about an hour after sunrise, once the day began to warm, Wayne would have one more thing to contend with.

We watched as he backed out of the driveway. He had the ziplock bag of ice pressed against his forehead and about a two-inch length of toilet paper extending from either nostril, which in the hazy light of dawn made him look even more ridiculous than normal. As Wayne drove off, he rolled down the window, honked twice, and gave us the finger.

"Well, what do you think?" Bonnie asked.

"Are you kidding, it's more like where to begin. You were married to that guy?"

"Oh, believe me, there isn't a day that goes by when I don't ask myself the same question. But no, I mean about his story, the guy giving him a hundred bucks. You think he was telling the truth?"

"I think the whole thing sounds so stupid it just might be true. With your software release coming up, I don't know. Maybe someone got wind of it. It suddenly makes some of Iggy's eccentrics look a little more sane. Obviously, I don't know Wayne at all, but the way he told that story about the hundred bucks some guy gave him at Benny's, I mean, that is so lame it almost has to be true."

"You mean they knew enough about me to know Wayne was my ex but didn't know I had a restraining order filed against him? Or, that he'd never, ever been here in his life? None of it seems to make any sense."

"Maybe Wayne convinced the guy he could get what he wanted. That's actually what we should be paying attention to, someone wanting the layout of this place. Sounds to me like they're planning to pay you a visit."

"Think they know about Iggy?" she asked.

"I would guess they do. If someone stole all his computers, wouldn't they essentially have the program? I mean, couldn't they take the thing and present it as their own?"

"I suppose, but we'd file a lawsuit, list the break-in, a robbery. I can't see anyone getting away with that."

"Unless you weren't around to file a lawsuit. Think about it."

"Oh."

"If someone had programmers and they had access to Iggy's computers, they could probably pull this off, right?"

"Possibly, yeah, sure."

"So maybe they just want to get access to the computers, not steal the things. Somehow take control of the programs and—"

"But we could still file a lawsuit and—"

"Like I said before, unless you weren't around to file."

Thirteen

I'd been nursing Cokes in a back booth at Benny's for the past three hours. I was thinking maybe I'd misjudged Bonnie's idiot ex, Wayne, when he suddenly stumbled in the front door apparently over-served and feeling no pain.

"What the hell happened to you?" the bartender asked, then drew a beer and slid it across the bar to Wayne. "On the house, man."

"Thanks, I don't know, I lost count, three or four of 'em, I think. Last night, just as I got home. I parked the truck, headed for the front door of the building when this one dude pops up, big bastard, asks me if I can lend him a dollar. I told him to get screwed, and the next thing I know, there's a bunch of 'em coming at me."

I couldn't see any toilet paper in his nostrils, but only because it had been replaced by a silver metal splint that covered his entire nose. It looked like it was edged in a blueish-green foam or rubber and taped to his face with white surgical tape. His nose sounded plugged, but that could have been due to the splint. The egg on his forehead was still in the shape of a perfect rectangle and had grown purple. Both eyes were swollen and black.

"Yeah, I took two or three of 'em out. It happened so fast I just lost count. Then one dude pulled a gun on me and said, 'I don't want no more trouble, you just get away from me, and I won't shoot.' I figured I had a couple of beers in the fridge up in my apartment, so I went inside."

"Oh, bullshit," some guy groaned from a couple of stools down the bar. Two other guys who'd been listening just shook their heads and walked back to their table.

"Give me that free beer back," the bartender said. Wayne grabbed the glass, stepped back, and immediately gulped down two thirds.

Some guy rose out of a booth, walked over to Wayne and put his arm around his shoulder, then guided Wayne down to the end of the bar. He was a good foot taller than Wayne with a hook nose and a wandering left eye. He was angular, all elbows, knees, bony shoulders, and wrists plus a bouncing Adam's apple. A receding hairline left him with what looked like a thinning mohawk. They seemed to be in a rather animated conversation. The guy poked Wayne in the chest with a bony index finger while Wayne shook his head and pointed to the metal splint covering his nose.

If I had to guess, I would have said the guy was looking for the layout to Bonnie's house or his hundred dollars back. Suddenly he pushed Wayne into a couple of empty stools and shouted, "A hundred bucks, asshole. Let's go."

"I told you, I don't have it. I deposited it in the bank last night."

"Bullshit, you were buying drinks all last night, you blew it, and then you didn't deliver. You…"

"Hey, fellas," the bartender yelled. "Take it outside. Go on, get out of here."

"I didn't do nothing. He's threatening me," Wayne pleaded.

The guy pushed Wayne again, and he half fell over a couple of bar stools.

"Okay, that's it. Both of you, get the hell out of here, now. Go on, get out, or I'm calling the cops."

The guy leaned forward, looked down at Wayne, and growled something. It was impossible to hear what he said, but I had a pretty good idea.

"I'm calling the cops," the bartender said and put a cellphone to his ear.

The guy glared, then hurried out the door. Wayne remained on the floor. I hurried out of my booth and headed toward the door. Wayne's swollen eyes grew wide when he recognized me.

"I, I, I didn't tell him nothing, honest, you can even ask him," he sputtered.

"I intend to do just that. And you better watch yourself, or I'll come looking for you. Got it?"

Wayne nodded meekly.

"Wayne," the bartender yelled. "This is your last warning, get the hell out of here, now. You're chasing away business."

Fourteen

A dark green Jaguar was pulling out of the parking lot as I stepped out of Benny's. The odd-looking guy who'd just pushed Wayne into the bar stools was behind the wheel of the Jag. Fortunately, he was focused on street traffic and didn't pay attention to me. The Jag took a right onto the street and drove off.

I jogged a half block to my car, jumped in, and prayed it would start. It did, and I sped off down the street in pursuit of the Jag. I was driving an '87 Lancer. It had originally been painted red, but with almost thirty years of fading, it was now various shades of pink. I spotted the Jag a few blocks later, then dropped back just far enough so a car could pull between us.

I followed him through downtown, then along West Seventh, until he took the 35-E entrance and headed south on the interstate. We drove for another ten minutes, through Mendota Heights and Eagan, where he took the Cedar Ave exit. Mercifully, another car was in front of me on the same exit. I followed at a discreet distance, saw him turn, and was about to do the same when I realized the street was just a cul-de-sac. I drove past, pulled over, then strolled back to the corner. I wrote down the address, and the license number of the Jag then pulled to the opposite side of the road and waited.

I checked in with Bonnie on my cellphone. Nothing out of the ordinary had happened. A little after nine that night, I drove home, packed a suitcase, and drove over to Bonnie's. She made me a couple of Iggy's hot dogs, and we sat out on the deck while Morton investigated the backyard.

"Thanks in advance for cleaning up after Morton," she said, then indicated him leaving a deposit back by the kid's sandbox.

"Oh, yeah, sorry about that. He was in the car with me for a few hours tonight. This is when we usually take a walk."

"Charming, just remember to clean it up, you can wait 'til morning if you want."

We chatted for another hour, then went to bed. Other than Morton poking me with his nose a half-dozen times, the rest of the night passed uneventfully.

Morton gave me a serious poke just before six the following morning and wouldn't stop until I climbed out of bed. I threw my clothes on and tiptoed out of the room. I let Morton out, put on a pot of coffee, then grabbed a shovel from the attached garage and cleaned up after him. I was just finishing my third mug of coffee when Bonnie strolled into the kitchen area.

She'd pulled on a terrycloth robe that was thick enough to hide all her attributes.

"Is there any coffee left?" she asked, then stood there scratching her head like she wasn't sure exactly where she was.

"Yeah, let me get you a cup. Can I make you breakfast?"

"You can in a bit. Let me get some coffee down first and see if I can wake up."

We didn't talk while she drank her coffee. As I refilled her mug, she said, "Did you think any more about what you're going to do with that idiot Wayne?"

"I don't think I'm going to do anything unless he comes around again, and then I think I'll just detain him and call the police."

"You mean, you're going to let him get away with it?"

"Get away with what?"

"Well, breaking in, for starters, and…"

"Actually, if you'll recall, he never got into the house. The only reason the door to the deck was open is because I unlocked it and then slid the thing open, and that was just so I could crack Wayne over the head. He got a goose egg on his forehead and his nose broken. He's in trouble to the tune of a hundred bucks with that skinny guy who pushed him down in Benny's. The way it looks to me, if we just leave him to his own devices, he'll probably keep screwing up and pissing people off. Not exactly the best plan for the future."

"I suppose," she said and sipped some coffee.

"Anything from downstairs?"

"You mean Iggy?"

"Is there anyone else down there in the dark?"

"Very funny. No, he sent a note out with his dinner dish last night. Said he felt a series of unusually strong electromagnetic pulses the other night and wondered if I was aware of anything."

"Really?"

Bonnie looked at me for a moment. "Dev, he probably heard something, and either stepped outside and watched or crept upstairs in the dark and watched."

"Other than you yelling a number of colorful things at Wayne, I didn't think we made that much noise."

"We didn't, but he often works through the night, I told you he's on some lunar schedule."

"Oh, yeah, the moon. How could I forget?"

"Well, like I said, it seems to work. What about that guy you followed?"

"The guy in the Jag? I've got a contact in the DMV. I'll call in the license number and find out who it's registered to. See if that links with the house address where it was parked and then take it from there."

"Then what will you do?"

"I'm not sure."

Fifteen

I phoned my contact in the Department of Motor Vehicles. We had our standard conversation, except she'd apparently been promoted and had a private office, so now she didn't have to whisper when she swore at me.

"Department of Motor Vehicles, how may I direct your call?"

"Donna Fenster, please, at extension three-three-one."

"One moment, please, and I'll connect…Oh, umm, I'm showing a Donna McCloud at that location. Does that sound right?"

I had no idea. "Yeah, sorry, my mistake, I think that's her."

"One moment, please, I'll connect you."

Donna answered on the third ring. "Department of Motor Vehicles, this is Donna. How may I help you?"

"Hey, Donna, long time no talk. I wonder if…"

"Gee, now just who did I piss off to get this call?"

"Hey, I don't know if I ever congratulated you on your promotion. Congratulations. I—"

"Thanks," she said, coming across as less than genuine. "Almost a year late, but thanks anyway. Now I can cross that off my list. Do I even need to ask why you're wasting my time on the phone?"

"The sooner you give me two tiny bits of information, the sooner I'm off your phone and out of your hair."

"And let me just save you the effort it will take to threaten me once again with exposure. Tell me what you need."

"First of all, what's with the name change? Did you remarry or go back to your maiden name?"

"None of your business. Now, I'm going to ask you one more time, and then I'm going to hang up if you don't tell me what you want."

"Okay, sorry, I tried to show an interest in your personal life and maybe move our relationship along, I—"

"Let me be very clear. We do not have a relationship. I'm warning you. You've got about five seconds left before I—"

"Can you look up this license number for me, please?" I said, trying to sound as nice as possible, and then I gave her the license number from the Jag.

"Hold on for a moment," she said, then half-whispered, "Bastard," before she put me on hold. She was back about a minute later. "Okay, you got a color crayon and a clean spot on the wall to write this down? Because I'm only going to tell you once. That's a 2016 'F' type model on the Jag, they go for around eighty grand if I'm not mistaken. Color is British Racing Green, does that sound right?"

"Yeah, I guess so. I mean, it's dark green."

"And you're supposed to be an investigator? My God. The vehicle is registered to a Niles Wegger. I suppose you want a home address."

"If it's not too much trouble."

"Will it get you off the phone?"

"Yes, give me a home address, and I'm gone."

"Oh, if only it were that simple. Niles Wegger, his residence is listed as…" then she read me the cul-de-sac address I'd written down last night. "One more thing, Mr. Haskell, listen closely. Asshole," she shouted and then hung up.

Nice to know I still had that effect on some people. In Donna's case, I'd caught her in a passionate relationship with an underage college intern some years back. I wasn't sure what the deal was with the different surname, not that I really cared. She still gave me the information I needed, and as long as I didn't call too often, I felt I would be able to hold her intern relationship over her head as long as she was employed by the DMV.

Based on the information I'd just received, Niles Wegger had driven home after threatening Wayne at Benny's. As far as I knew, he remained home for the evening. Time to find out what I could about the man.

Sixteen

I phoned Bonnie first. She answered with, "Yeah, Dev, what is it?" sounding rushed.

"Hey, Bonnie, sorry to bother you. The name Niles Wegger ring a bell with you?"

"No, no, not really. Why, should it?"

"Too soon to tell, apparently that's the guy that shoved Wayne at Benny's, the guy I followed home. I'm just beginning to check some things out. I was going to send Iggy an email, but I don't have his address, could you…?"

"Don't bother emailing him. It will just drop into his junk file. He's got about a dozen different security set-ups, not to mention the one he wrote. Were you going to ask him about that name? This Wegger guy?"

"Yeah, as a matter of fact."

"You mind if I just ask him? Probably get you an answer that much faster."

"No, please do."

"Good, you're here tonight, right?'

"That okay with you?"

"More than okay. Sorry if I was a drag last night. I'll make it up to you tonight."

"You don't have to do…"

"No offense, but I was thinking of my needs just now. If you feel guilty, you could go ahead and bring dinner again."

"I will, and we can have a relaxing night. I'll see you a little after seven if that's okay."

"More than okay, it's perfect."

"What are you hungry for?"

"Other than my earlier request? Go ahead and surprise me. I'm cooking hot dogs for Iggy, so don't worry about him."

"See you around seven," I said and hung up. It gave me the better part of the day to see what I could learn about scrawny Niles Wegger.

* * *

"Yeah, Niles Wegger, I looked him up after you called," Wendy said, then took a sip from her glass of Chardonnay.

We were sitting in Kincaid's, one of the more trendy restaurants in town, which maybe explained why I wasn't in here all that often. A few years back, Wendy and I had a romance that lasted no more than a couple of weeks. We'd been pulled over for Driving Under the Influence. Wendy was behind the wheel. Fortunately, an old hockey buddy was the officer that pulled us over and, since I was in the passenger seat and Wendy only lived four blocks away, he made us turn over the keys and walk home. We picked up the keys at the station the following morning. Wendy was forever thankful for my involvement and, at the same time, blamed me for being even more intoxicated than she was. Since she worked for the Attorney General's office, continued association with me seemed to not be in the best interest of her career. Over time we eventually became friends again.

"He's a pretty slippery guy. Probably worked a number of scams around the world, through a bunch of intermediaries."

"Around the world?"

"Yeah. That's not as big a deal as it sounds with today's online opportunities. He was suspected of being connected to various scams coming out of India, Pakistan, Russia, Estonia, Brazil. He can do it all from his kitchen counter. He doesn't actually have to travel there.

"Was he arrested? Did he serve time?"

"No, nothing like that. There are so many versions and angles these guys run, not to mention the sheer layers we'd have to go through to get them. We have all we can handle just trying to catch the crooks here."

"But you just said he didn't travel to any of these places."

"Yeah, and I also said he was suspected. But nothing we could prove conclusively."

"So, what exactly is he suspected of doing?"

She looked over her shoulder and scanned the room. "Not like it's an ongoing investigation or anything, but I still shouldn't be telling you this."

"I just want to know about the guy. But if what you tell me has any connection to my clients, I'll tell you, and it might turn out to be the kind of investigation you could hang your hat on."

She seemed to think about that for a moment and drained her glass. The bartender stepped in front of us and gave a questioning look. I nodded, and he went to get another glass of Chardonnay and a beer for me.

"I probably shouldn't," Wendy said, then waited until the fresh glass was delivered, and she took a sip.

"So, Niles Wegger?" I asked.

"Okay. He's a local guy. Studied at the U. Did grad work at MIT and before that something at Carnegie Mellon. You have to be a real egghead to get in those places. Rumor is he went from MIT to some government thing."

"Government thing?"

"I don't know. We basically got an access denied reply from the feds."

"The State Attorney General's office was told access denied?"

"Yeah, happens more than you'd care to know. Well, that is until some sort of problem becomes public, and then it's suddenly our fault or local law enforcement."

I was thinking of Iggy. Bonnie had said that he'd worked for some department in the government with a big acronym. "So you've no idea what government agency he worked for?"

"No, but that's not really here nor there, well, except it might suggest a skill level, a particular capability. The things we attempted to link him to, along with a dozen other states, were a number of fake tech scams."

"Fake tech scams?"

"Yeah, there are, or were, a number of different versions. One would be a recording that suddenly comes across your screen with maybe a sign flashing that says 'Warning,' and it gives you a number to call. Another version is some guy calls you and says he's from Microsoft or Windows or someplace, and they've received an alert that your security has been breached."

I took a sip of my beer and thought about that for a moment. "I'm not a real savvy computer guy."

"Except on the porn sites. Remember, you showed me that one."

"Oh, yeah, but I was just looking around online and ran across that one."

"Yeah, sure you did. Anyway, the scam, people call the number or talk to the guy if someone called them. They have you download a program, some remote desktop software that gives them access to your computer and allows them to gather all sorts of personal information. Then they try and scam you into paying a couple hundred bucks for a security package that's probably already on your computer."

"And Niles Wegger is suspected of making these calls."

"No, he's way up the food chain. They've got minimum wage geeks making the call from India or wherever. We suspect he's scammed folks out of millions over the years. He'd set the thing up somewhere outside of the US, then shut it down after a short amount of time and start up the next day from somewhere else in the world. They call using a voiceover IP that costs them absolutely nothing and hides their identity. They can call you from absolutely anywhere in the world."

"If Wegger set this up, can't you nail him?"

"We've been unable to sufficiently link him to any of this and frankly don't have the technology or the staff. He'd have to get charged by the feds, and then we would probably ride on their coattails. Anyway, that's about it on my end. What do you have for me?"

"Something equally as vague, maybe." I went on to tell her about Bonnie and Iggy and the software they planned to release. I told her about Wayne and his failed break-in and his brief conversation with Niles Wegger the following evening.

"So, based on Wegger shouting something about a hundred bucks, you figure he wanted a layout of this woman's house?"

"Yeah. The idiot that tried to break in—"

"This Wayne guy, her ex-husband."

"Yeah, he said someone gave him a hundred bucks, cash. Then Wegger is yelling about it the following night."

"Kind of thin," she said and took a sip of wine.

"Well, the other thing is this Iggy character, the guy wrapped in tinfoil. He told Bonnie that he worked for some government agency, a department with some long acronym name. Maybe it's that top-secret joint where Wegger worked."

"Hmmm-mmm. This Iggy person, what's his full name?"

"God, I never thought to ask."

"And you're the private investigator?"

"Yeah, I know."

Seventeen

Morton and I showed up promptly at seven with dinner and two bottles of wine. Morton had already been walked and fed, not that he wouldn't beg at the table.

"Thank God," Bonnie said when she opened the door. She tore the bottles of wine from my hand. "Come on. I'm literally starving, afraid I was going to waste away."

I followed her up the stairs carrying the bag from Fat Daddy's, the rib place in the same building as my office. "I got you a nice salad."

She turned and stared at me for a moment. "A salad? Do you have any idea what my day has been like? You better be carrying more than a salad in that bag, Mister, or you're on the couch tonight, and Morton can have your place in the bed."

"Just kidding, my little bird-dropping, I brought you ribs, from Fat Daddy's."

"Ribs? Okay, you're back in my good graces, at least temporarily, and I'll just forget that little bird shit remark."

She had calmed substantially halfway through her first glass of wine. It was a gorgeous, still evening, just the right temperature with birds chirping their 'good night' songs. We were sitting out on the deck, chewing on delicious ribs and eating coleslaw from a shared container. The sun was almost down, and Morton was under the table gnawing on a bone that Bonnie had given him when she thought I wasn't looking.

"I never asked you Iggy's full name."

"Iggy? I think he goes by Iggy almost exclusively. I've never seen anything official like a driver's license or a passport. I don't know about a passport, but I'm pretty sure he doesn't have a license. Tell you the truth, I don't even know if he can drive."

"So, you don't know his actual name?"

"Oh, yeah, it's Ignatius Arnold. But I've always referred to him as Iggy."

"How is his mail addressed?"

"What mail? He's never gotten any."

"Never— How can that be? Everyone gets mail. Even if it's just junk mail."

"I don't recall ever seeing any for him. Think about it. He's a supercomputer nerd. He lives here. What expenses does he have?"

"But doesn't he have a bank account or insurance or something?"

"Not that I'm aware of, Dev, he's a computer nerd. He does all that stuff online. I mean, no offense, but he just might be a little more tech-savvy than you or even me. Hey, pass me that plate of ribs, God, these things are good."

"So did you ask him about Niles Wegger?" I asked as I passed the ribs to her.

"Yeah, I'd love to tell you he gave me a strange look, but we were talking to one another through the closed door. I just thought there was a funny or maybe a surprised tone in his voice, but I couldn't be sure."

"What did he say?"

"Umm, he just said he'd have to get back to me. Why, who is he?"

"I did some checking today. Turns out, that's the name of the guy I think gave Wayne the hundred bucks to get a layout of your home. I talked to someone I know in the Attorney General's office, and they have a file on him, although they've never charged or prosecuted the guy. They suspect he's created all sorts of computer scams, stealing personal information and stuff. The interesting thing is that he worked for some top-secret government department or agency, and not even the Attorney General's office could get info on what it was."

"Like that long acronym Iggy mentioned?"

"That's kind of what I was thinking, maybe the same place. I don't know. But if you make some assumptions, some high tech scammer finds out Iggy is working on this project for you. Maybe he wants to steal it, your software."

"No," Bonnie said, shaking her head.

"What do you mean, no?"

"Think big, Dev. What if he doesn't steal it, but instead, he just puts some bug in there that would let him collect personal information, credit cards, bank accounts, passwords. Then the thing goes out to every household in the nation. It could turn out to be a real mess. Hey, are you going to eat those last couple of ribs?"

"Help yourself. You seem to be rather laid back about the potential disaster you might have on your hands."

"That's because I have all the faith in the world in Iggy. Well, and you, too, keeping us safe. I mean, you got that dumb shit, Wayne, the other night."

"Yeah, but this Wegger guy is at a little higher level. Makes Wayne look like he's on the bench for a little league team, and this guy is MVP for the majors."

"Except Iggy is even better than that. I should have brought some paper towels out. You want some hand wipes?"

"God, after gnawing on about ten pounds of ribs, I should probably hit the shower."

"Great idea, there's room for both of us. I'll get the water going while you clean up the table. Don't take too long."

"Not to worry," I said, then cleaned up in record time and hurried to the shower.

Eighteen

We showered and then climbed into bed. It was everything I'd hoped for and more if that was possible. Morton's growl woke me from my post-coital sleep around three. He didn't bark but just let off a steady growl as he stood by the door. He glanced over at me as I sat up, gave me a look that suggested, 'Come on, get going.' I slipped on my boxers and grabbed my pistol off the nightstand. Bonnie was breathing deeply, almost snoring, but not quite with the pillow half over her head.

We tiptoed cautiously down the hallway. Morton moved in a particular creep, almost like he was stalking a bird. I heard a sound that seemed to be coming from the kitchen, and I relaxed a bit, thinking it would be Iggy cooking a hotdog or something. Suddenly, a beam of light came on just long enough to flash on the staircase, heading down to the front door level before it flicked off.

Morton's growl became a lot more audible, and whoever held the flashlight clicked it back on and illuminated Morton. This time he barked, took two steps forward and barked again. I stepped to the side, still somewhat behind him, although I could see his teeth were bared.

"Shit," a voice said from behind the light and started to back up. "Easy, nice doggie, easy."

I flicked on the light switch, illuminating the living room, the kitchen, and the deck outside. A wide-eyed skinny guy stood staring back at me. It wasn't Niles Wegger, although there was a definite resemblance. This guy was just as skinny and at least as unattractive, if not more so. "Shit. I'm, I'm sorry, I must have the wrong house."

Morton barked, then growled, but remained where he was. I raised my pistol and said, "I think it would be a good idea if you got down on your knees and put your hands behind your head."

"Look, I'm awfully sorry, I seem to have made a terrible mistake. Now, if I could just—"

"Your first mistake was breaking in here. The second one was not doing what I told you to do." Morton barked again.

"Does he bite?" The guy sounded more frightened of Morton than of me holding a pistol.

"He only bites if I tell him to, in which case he'll rip a very large piece out of you. And once he tastes blood. Well…" Morton barked, and then as if on command, he took a step forward.

"Just keep him there, mister."

"Then get down on your knees, now, or he's going to tear your hand off. I promise," I said, and the guy quickly dropped to his knees. He set the flashlight on the floor, a small black thing maybe as big around as a quarter and about four inches long. He quickly placed his hands behind his head and watched Morton out of the corner of his eye.

"Who the hell are you?"

"I told you, I'm a neighbor. From the next street over," he added quickly. "I seemed to have made a mistake and I—"

"You've got about two seconds to start telling the truth before I shoot you and call the cops."

"I just told you, I—"

I placed both hands around the pistol grips, then assumed a dramatic pose and aimed at his head. I could see him swallow nervously. He cringed and leaned backward in an effort to get further away from the pistol, but he didn't say anything. I lowered the pistol and aimed at his crotch.

"Okay, okay. God, please don't shoot. Jesus, please. God, I knew this was a stupid idea right from the get-go. I was supposed to be in and out of here in sixty seconds. Now look, I'm screwed."

"What were you going to do that would only take sixty seconds?"

"Iggy. We have no way of contacting him. He's changed all his email addresses, basically disappeared from online view, we can't locate his system. We just wanted to get in touch with him."

"So you thought breaking in was the way to go? Why not just ring the doorbell during daylight hours?"

He seemed to think about that for a moment, at least long enough to know he hadn't convinced me. There was a six-foot extension cord on the floor behind him running along the wall from a socket to a table lamp. "So let me ask you again, why didn't you just ring the doorbell?" I said, then stepped past him, pulled the extension cord out of the socket, and unplugged the lamp.

I wrapped the cord around his wrist, then pulled his arms behind his back, tied his wrists one to the other, then tied the cord around one of his ankles. All the while, I kept telling Morton not to bite. Morton looked at me like he couldn't figure out what I was saying. Once the guy was bound, Morton walked over and licked his face.

"I think he's just seeing if he'd like the taste. He can move fast, and I should warn you, he hasn't been fed for almost twelve hours."

"Oh, God, come on, man, I didn't do anything. Please," he whined.

"Well, unfortunately, I have the feeling you're not being very truthful. You broke in here to get an email address? How stupid do I look?"

He seemed to think about that for a moment, so I said, "The name Niles Wegger mean anything?" A look of resignation slowly washed over his face.

"You already know about him?"

"Of course," I said. "We've been working nonstop on a special program just for him. I'm a little surprised you don't know about it, but then, Niles never did turn out to be as bright as everyone said he was. Always a bit of a disappointment."

"And a jerk, you can add that in there, too."

"Oh, yeah, a real jerk," I said.

"He didn't even know anything about you or your guard dog."

"Believe me, that's not going to be his biggest…"

The guy suddenly whipped the extension cord at me, then was up, on his feet, and running out the sliding door. I pointed my pistol at him, but I didn't pull the trigger. He leaped over the deck railing, and I waited for the screams and cries when he landed but didn't hear any-thing. A moment later, I saw him running across the backyard and then between two houses and onto the next street. I thought I detected a bit of a limp, but he was still moving pretty fast, probably expecting Morton to bite him at any moment. Morton was otherwise occupied, standing at the kitchen counter and looking up at his food dish. I was barefoot, in my boxers, and not about to give chase.

I picked up the little flashlight and set it on the kitchen counter, then poured some dog food into Mor-ton's dish. I grabbed the plate with a couple of smoked ribs out of the refrigerator and sat down at the counter. Morton glanced at his dish, then gave a woeful glance at my plate of ribs. "Don't even think about it, Morton."

Nineteen

Bonnie was leaning against the kitchen counter, wearing just a t-shirt. A very short t-shirt, oblivious. "That's it? You just sat here eating the rest of those smoked ribs in your underwear and let him get away?"

"What? You want me to shoot the guy?"

"Well, yeah, for starters."

She was sipping a cup of coffee and in the process of reading me the riot act. "I mean, the guy broke in here, Dev. By the way, how did he even get in? Wayne couldn't get in."

"Wayne's an idiot."

"You don't have to tell me," she said, then slurped more coffee. "But, I mean, did he actually pick the lock? And even if he did—"

Oh-oh. She had stopped in mid-sentence and seemed to suddenly be deep in thought.

"I always put that board behind the door before I go to bed so the door won't slide and—" She looked at me for a very long moment. "Wait a minute. You said you'd wash up in here last night."

"And I did, I even put things away."

"Did you bother to lock the door? God, did you even think to close it?"

"I might have had some other things on my mind."

"I don't believe it. You can't be that…"

"Hey, don't blame me. If you weren't so good, so fantastic, I…"

"Just stop right there. God, Dev, we could all be dead. You're supposed to be the security specialist." She flared her eyes and slurped more coffee.

"That's your term, not mine. Besides, it worked out okay. I mean, no one got hurt."

"Luckily. No thanks to you."

"I'm the one who scared him off. You managed to sleep through it all with a smile on your face after your workout in the shower and again in bed."

"I don't recall you complaining."

"Maybe we should head back to…"

"Dev," she screamed just as I began to reach forward.

"Okay, okay. Sorry, I was just trying to get you calmed down and—"

"Yeah, that's what you were thinking about, me. Give me a break."

"It couldn't hurt."

"Will you, just for once, try and think about something else? It doesn't always have to be about sex. God," she said, then drained her coffee cup and held the empty out for a refill.

"I'm a guy. It's the way we're wired."

"Dev, stop it," she shouted. If she mentioned going to bed and just talking about how our day went, I was out the door.

"Security, Dev, protection. It's why you're here."

I switched gears. "Okay, I'd say we've established the fact that this Niles guy and whoever else is with him wants whatever it is he thinks you have."

"What?"

"I'm guessing he has some rough ideas, but he probably isn't a hundred percent sure what you and Iggy have been working on. You've contacted potential clients, right?"

"A couple of the big names, setting up appointments, but I've been purposefully vague, nonspecific until I can meet with them in person."

"Maybe Wegger has contacts at some level. Maybe Iggy unwittingly gave them information. The one thing, actually a couple of things last night's episode confirms, is that they aren't about to give up. They have some vague idea of what you're doing, and they seem to be more interested in Iggy, or at least his program and not you."

She nodded as she poured more coffee, then sipped from the fresh mug. "Plus, they didn't know about you being here."

"Yeah, and they may just think I was here for a sleepover instead of security."

"That's why you left the door open? To fool them?"

"You believe that?" I said, sounding hopeful.

"No, and from now on, I'll be in charge of locking up."

"Fair enough. I think it might be time for me to pay Niles Wegger a visit."

"Do you think that's such a good idea? What are you going to say? What do you hope to find out?"

"I won't know until after the visit."

"Hmmm, let me think about that."

"Bonnie, what's to think about? The guy who ran out of here last night, I'm about ninety-nine percent sure he ran straight to Wegger and told him exactly what happened. Next time they try to come in here, and there will be a next time, they're going to do it forcefully, take whatever they want, whether it's programs, computers, Iggy or all of the above. Doesn't it make more sense to cut them off at the pass? At least maybe give them a second thought that it's not the best idea?"

Twenty

When I drove over to the cul-de-sac, the green Jaguar was parked in the driveway, looking like it hadn't moved since the last time I saw it. I pulled in behind, turned off the Lancer, then sat there behind the wheel while the stupid Lancer coughed and sputtered, deciding whether or not it was going to shut down. Once it stopped, I climbed out. I thought I might have caught a slight movement from a window shade but couldn't be sure, not that it made any difference. I walked to the front door, a solid-looking, black-metal thing, and rang the doorbell, then stepped back and smiled up at the security camera mounted above the door. After a long moment, I gave a little finger wave at the camera.

"What's this about?" a voice said from somewhere.

"I'd like to talk to Niles Wegger," I said, looking up at the camera.

"Regarding?"

I pulled the small flashlight from my pocket, turned it on, and pointed it at the camera. "If Mr. Wegger is too busy, my next stop is the police."

There was a pause and then a loud buzz, followed by a lock clicking on the front door. I turned the handle, and the front door opened, so I stepped in. The metal door led into a small entry with another door. This door had a large panel of leaded glass in floral pattern with beveled glass on the outside edges of the panel. There was a large staircase on the far wall with someone coming down the stairs who looked an awful lot like Niles Wegger. He gave a friendly wave like we were long lost pals, then walked across the oak floor of the foyer and opened the door. "You must be Devlin Haskell," he smiled and extended his hand, all charm, and affability.

I shook his hand, didn't ask how he knew my name and said, "Yes, and you're Niles Wegger, it's nice to finally meet you." I tried to look him in the eye, but with that wandering left eye, I wasn't sure exactly where to focus.

"What can I do for you?"

I reached back into my pocket and pulled out the small flashlight. "I believe someone you know may have left this earlier this morning while in the process of making a surprise visit."

His Adam's apple, about the size of a golf ball, bobbed up and down three or four times. "That's nice, but I don't think it would have been anyone I know."

"That's not what he told me at three this morning while I had a pistol drawn on him."

"Under those circumstances, I'm sure people would say just about anything. But where are my manners?

Please, won't you join me in the library?" he said and extended a hand down a hallway. "That door on your left."

I headed down the hallway past a series of professionally-taken photos of the house that were framed and hanging along the wall. My eyes were busy flashing left and right, expecting someone to suddenly jump out. Fortunately, nothing happened, and Wegger suddenly said, "This room here."

The room was a modest size, not particularly large, but certainly not small. A red and blue oriental rug that appeared antique and expensive covered most of the oak floor. Two windows on the far wall looked out onto the front lawn and the driveway. My Lancer, parked behind the gleaming green Jag, looked even worse from this distance. Two of the walls held shoulder-high, built-in oak bookcases. On the end wall was a fireplace with a built-in bookcase on either side and an antique mirror over the mantel. The shelves of the bookcases were filled with leather-bound books, a number of them looking very old.

A wide, mahogany desk with an inlaid leather surface sat in front of the fireplace, and as Wegger stepped behind the desk, he said, "Please, have a seat," indicating one of two antique leather chairs in front of the desk. Two large computer screens were mounted on either side of the desk, Wegger sat between them. For a brief moment, I thought of Iggy, the only difference being this room was bright.

I pulled a chair back and sat down. Wegger settled into his black office chair and studied me for a long moment before he finally spoke. "So, what's it gonna take?"

"I'm not sure I'm following."

"You. No doubt it's why you're here. Right? What's it gonna take to get you on my side?"

"Your side? I guess I'm in the dark here. You had two guys attempt to break into Bonnie's, both turned out to be unsuccessful. You apparently…"

"Two?"

"Yeah, your guy last night, the one limping around today, and that idiot Wayne a night or two before. Wore an attractive nose splint, had two black eyes and a lump on his forehead the night you pushed him into a bunch of bar stools at Benny's."

"Well done. I may have underestimated you. Tell me what you know about Iggy Arnold."

His wandering eye was getting to me, so I focused on the bookshelf behind him. "Iggy, I know the two of you worked together in, how should I put it? Government security?"

He nodded. "Yes. I worked with Iggy long enough to know he has a variety of concerns. He's a little paranoid, thinks the highway department is trying to scan his brain along with a few dozen other issues, but at the end of the day, he's still a genius. Now, what's it gonna take to get you on board? Come on, level with me. If you weren't interested, you wouldn't be sitting in that chair right now. Correct?"

"The only reason I'm sitting in this chair is to warn you about trying anything else. Next time I catch someone in there, and I will catch them, but next time I'm not going to let them off. I'm going to hurt them, and then I'm going to come looking for you. Believe me, you don't want that, and I certainly don't want that."

He gave a small laugh, then said, "I think you've seen far too many movies, Haskell. But what if, just for the sake of discussion, what if I could offer you enough money so you'd never, ever have to work again? You could just relax, take it easy, never have another worry, for the rest of your life. I have to believe something like that would interest you. Make you think maybe it was worth the risk. Except that, I forgot to mention, there is no risk. It's all scot-free, more money than you ever dreamed. All you have to do is sit on your ass, hold your hand out and get paid."

"Sounds great. Unfortunately, I've already got a job, and I intend to see it through."

"Yes, your current form of employment. Hitting people over the head with a board, wrapping someone up with an extension cord, showering with a sex-crazed blonde…"

"She's not a natural blonde," I said, hoping I was able to hide my surprise.

"I'm aware of that fact," he said, raising his voice. He paused for a moment, regaining control, then took a deep breath and continued. "You're working for a certifiable individual, wrapped in tinfoil, who thinks the highway department is using electromagnetic fields to scan his brain. Not to mention his partner, a woman who's betting on her good looks and a prayer that she can sell a revolutionary software package to the largest retailer in the world."

"Yeah, I guess that pretty much sums it up."

"Tell me, do you have connections on the police force?" Wegger asked as I got out of my chair.

"I have some favorite arresting officers."

"Better tell them to get ready. You leave my offer on the table, and you may just find yourself in a heap of trouble."

"Interesting, and here I thought I was going to go the extra mile just by warning you." I picked the flashlight up from his desk and shoved it into my pocket.

"I thought you were returning that."

"Yeah, that was the intention, but on second thought, I think I'll just hang onto it. Don't underestimate me, Wegger, and stay away from Iggy and Bonnie."

He half-laughed, "I can get whatever I want, sitting right here."

"Enjoy your day, pleasure meeting you. You got a pretty nice joint here. Hey, don't get up, I'll see myself out."

His face grew red, his Adam's apple bobbed up and down like a basketball, and that left eye seemed to roll up into his head as he watched me leave the room. On the way out, I counted two more security cameras, one in the hallway and one on the staircase. I let myself out the front door, thought about leaving the door open, but, ever the gentleman, I closed it behind me.

I climbed in the Lancer and attempted to start it. The thing finally coughed to life on the third try. I revved the engine a couple of times to make sure it was going to stay alive, casting a large blue cloud of exhaust across the cul-de-sac in the process. As I pulled away, I noticed a large oil slick the size of a dinner plate on the driveway behind the Jag compliments of my Lancer. Nice to meet you, Wegger.

Twenty-one

I'd been knocking on Iggy's locked door for the past ten minutes. I wanted to let him know what had transpired so he could prepare himself for whatever Wegger had planned. I was sure Wegger was going to try something. I just hoped Iggy could tell me what it was. "Come on, Iggy, open up, we need to talk."

I could hear him moving around on the other side of the door, heard his Mylar blanket rustling in the dark. It dawned on me once again that the guy was certifiable, and this was who I was hanging my hat on since Bonnie was gone for the afternoon.

"Iggy, come on, man, don't make me kick in the door."

"You, you wouldn't do that, Dev. Would you?" he called, not sounding all that sure about me.

"I'm putting my door kicking boots on as we speak, Iggy. I'm going to kick in that door, and then when I do, well, the highway department will just have an easier time for any scanning they might want to do."

I heard muttering from the other side but couldn't make out what was being said.

"Iggy, I'm pretty much out of time, so I'm going to count to three. If you don't unlock the door, I'm going to kick it in. Here we go. One. Two. Three. Hey, did you hear me? I said three, Iggy, three."

Still no response. I slammed the palm of my hand against the door, hoping it would sound like a kick from inside Iggy's cave.

"All right, all right, just a moment, don't kick it again," he shouted from the other side, then unsnapped the lock. A moment later, the door opened. "Okay, okay, but hurry in before they're aware of the breach. Come on, hurry, hurry, please."

I hustled into the dark, and Iggy quickly slammed the door behind me, hitting the back of my heel. He snapped the lock and then wedged a chair up beneath the doorknob.

"Thanks for letting me in, Iggy. I know you…"

"It's not like you gave me much of a choice. They monitor my defensive perimeter constantly. I can only hope they weren't able to breach it. I'll know in just a moment," he said, then rustled past me and sat down in front of another bank of computers I hadn't recalled seeing on my previous visit. He rapidly ran his fingers over the keyboard, issuing a series of commands, then pulled the Mylar sheet tighter around his shoulders and braced himself as he read the screen.

"Look, Iggy, while you're checking on your defensive perimeter, I don't know how aware you are of what's been going on here the last couple of evenings."

"You mean you and Bonnie? Pounding and riding one another through the night? Rather impossible not to miss the activity. Relax, the system automatically destroys the images after twenty-four hours, well, unless I override that capability."

"You-you've got video of us, too?"

"And audio," he said, then paused. "You mean Bonnie records her activities?"

"Bonnie? No, but Niles Wegger knew," I said, without going into specifics.

He didn't seem too surprised and asked, "Are you going to tell her I've recorded both of you?"

"How much upstairs do you have under surveillance?"

"How much? Why, everything, of course." I detected a slight smile illuminated by the computer screen.

"And outside?"

"Enough to keep everyone safe."

I moved on. "So, what did you see regarding our last two visitors?"

"Well, the one you assaulted, Wayne, I was alerted a good ten minutes before you interceded. As a matter of fact, I was about to phone the police when you pulled the door open and introduced yourself. Well done, I might add."

"Thank you. What about the guy last night?"

"The perimeter alarm wasn't activated because someone left that sliding door open. He just walked right in. It wasn't until the voice activation kicked in that I was made aware of anything."

"And you have an image, a recording?"

"I thought you might be asking that. I've already reproduced an image. I ran it on both the local and national databases. I have a match, ninety-seven-point-nine on the national base, and ninety-nine-point-three on the local base. You can just round that up to a hundred percent certainty. It came up Delmar Wegger on both databases, although I could have told you that without running it through the database. I've met him two or three times. He's the younger brother of Niles."

"You know this?"

"It was my job, and I took it very seriously. Niles was, at one time, a trustworthy member of our team. Unfortunately, he became enamored with the financial potential of our work and, well, that's why he finds himself where he is today."

"And where is that?"

"On the outside looking in."

"So you guys were part of a team that worked for a government agency. What was it the FBI, the CIA, NSA?"

"I'm really not at liberty to discuss that."

"Sorry, I asked. But let me ask you this, what can we expect from your former colleague, Niles Wegger?"

"You mean after your meeting with him this morning?"

"How did you know about that?"

"I was there, listening."

"What?"

"I was there, in his computer. He has two somewhere in that room. It's a rather simple procedure to hack in and utilize a microphone. I can tape things and then listen twenty-four hours later if I choose. Although I listened to the two of you, live this morning."

"But how did you ever get in there? Into Wegger's library?"

"I did it from a remote location. It's relatively simple. Anyone can do it, even you. Well, maybe."

"You haven't seen me in action. I can screw up Windows faster…"

"Just for a start, I use Linux. It allows me to turn off their antivirus system, embed a software key logger and—"

"You know, if the lights were on in this place, you'd be able to see my eyes spinning opposite ways right now."

Iggy actually laughed, or was it a groan? I wasn't sure. Then he said, "You know he wasn't kidding, Wegger. He meant what he said. You could go with him and never have to work another day in your life."

"Yeah, and all I'd have to do is live with the fact that I let him rip off you and Bonnie, two people who trusted me, for the rest of my life. No thanks. I'm just not wired that way."

Iggy stared at me in the dark for a long moment, then said, "They'll be returning, although not today. Bonnie's scheduled to fly out to Seattle tomorrow. They'll be back once she's gone."

"Do you know who? How many? And while we're at it, if you can record conversations from Wegger's library, how come they can't do the same thing here? Why do they even have to break in?"

"I have a number of VPN's established, and they change every twenty-three minutes. It makes it virtually impossible to…"

"Wait a minute, back up, what the hell is a VPN?"

Iggy gave a long sigh. "VPN stands for virtual private network. I have a number of them that change regularly. It's basically like a large safe where some aspect of the combination changes every few minutes. It's simple yet impossible to hack. Therefore, they have to gain physical access, imbed their program, and depart without my knowledge. It's why we've had the last two break-ins. It's why I've locked myself down here for the past six months. Ultimately, it's why Bonnie contacted you."

"Why not just get some armed guards or move everything in the dead of night?"

"Armed guards bring attention and, even if we moved, they would be able to track us. On the one hand, it's quite complex, but then on the other, it's pretty basic. Here, look at this," he said, then clicked about a hundred keys in just a second or two. All sorts of lines of computer code and things I had no idea what they were began scrolling across the screen.

"See, just a simple click of the keys and look at the information."

"It looks like an algebra problem from high school. What the hell does it mean?" I said.

Another sigh. "It's his position, Niles Wegger."

"Position? Like he's sitting down or standing?"

"No," he sighed again as if to say 'I don't believe it.' "No, this is his location, where he's at, the specific geographic coordinates. If I click here, insert some code," he clicked another fifty or sixty keys. "I can see his position, apparently a Super America station out on Pilot Knob road. I'd guess he's refueling his vehicle."

"Getting gas."

"Yes, Mr. Haskell, he's getting gas."

"And you say we've got until tomorrow night?"

"To the best of my knowledge. However, while we know a lot about Mr. Wegger, we are rather limited when it comes to those in his employ. If he meets with an individual, say in a restaurant or a park…"

"Or a bar?"

"Yes, or a bar, it's quite possible we would have no knowledge of such a meeting. Do you understand?"

I sat there thinking for a long moment.

"Mr. Haskell?"

"Yeah, I get it, sounds like we're kind of screwed."

"Hmmm, I guess in so many words, that could quite possibly be the scenario."

"I'm thinking I might get some help. Maybe just to keep things a little more even. Then, with you listening in and all the early warning stuff, well maybe we got a chance."

"Time will tell," Iggy said, then clicked another bunch of keys and sat there watching the computer gibberish run across the screen. "One more thing before you go," he said.

I was out of the chair and heading to where I thought the door might be. "Yeah?"

"His warning about the police. I wouldn't ignore that. He'll do something. Use your email to send threats to the President or attempt to misappropriate funds from a major charity. Something newsworthy that will cause an immediate reaction and can be traced to you."

"Not to worry, my computer is turned off," I said.

Iggy gave an audible sigh. "That doesn't really matter. Please be careful."

Twenty-two

I placed a call to Dog Colli, hoping he'd be able to help, but got dumped into his message center. Then, against my better judgment, I called Luscious Dixon. Luscious was a former NFL tight end for three different teams and never played a game. His anger management issues, along with the felony convictions, proved to be a little more than the revamped, caring, sensitive NFL wanted to deal with. It was close to two in the afternoon when I called, and I had the distinct impression I woke him up.

"Mmmm, what?" a sleepy voice growled.

"Luscious, Dev Haskell, catch you at a bad time?"

"Dev? Oh-oh, what time is it?"

"Almost two."

"Damn, missed that job interview."

"Want me to call back, or do you need a ride somewhere?"

"No, too late, it was s'posed to be at nine this morning. That's okay, didn't want the job anyway."

"You looking for work?"

"Not really. My mom lined it up. She's always got ideas about how I should spend my time."

'Yeah, imagine the nerve, wanting her son to get a job,' I thought. "Well, I might be able to use a man of your…capabilities. Nothing too stressful, just keeping an eye on things."

"Are meals included?"

"I think I can find a way to do that. You interested?"

"When do I start?"

"Well, I was thinking the sooner, the better. You want to grab a shower? I could pick you up in an hour or so."

"Oh, I can skip the shower, maybe pick me up in a half-hour. Then we could stop at McDonalds if that's okay?"

At close to four hundred pounds, Luscious skipping a shower didn't seem like the best idea. "How 'bout this, you hop in the shower, I'll grab the McDonalds on the way and meet you in an hour, sound okay?"

"Perfect," he said, and we hung up.

Between the Big Macs, double cheeseburgers, three large orders of fries, and three large strawberry shakes, it was close to a fifty dollar bill. On the other hand, a small price to pay for the security. No one was getting past Luscious. I could just place him in a chair in the middle of the sliding door, and the rear entrance would be effectively blocked. You'd need a forklift to move him. I pulled in front of his building about an hour later. He was already out there waiting for me.

Not exactly an attractive image, he was sitting in the middle of the steps leading up to the front door. Luscious was perfectly placed to be in the way of anyone with an idea of coming or going, and in the process of finishing the remnants of a giant Butterfinger candy bar. Another wrapper lay at his feet. I honked as I pulled the Lancer to the curb, then lowered the window.

"Hey, Lucious, good to see you, man. Hop in back. There'll be more room, and the McDonald's are all back there."

He crammed the last of the Butterfinger into his mouth, licked his fingertips so as not to miss a crumb, then reached up and grabbed the wrought iron railing, pulling himself to his feet. The railing wobbled back and forth but somehow managed to remain attached to the steps and the wall of the building.

I reached over the seat and unlocked the back door just as Luscious pulled the handle. He backed into the Lancer, and gradually inched his way across the rear seat, shaking the car back and forth, like it had just been hit by a series of tidal waves from either side. "Good to see you, Dev. Now, where are those McDonald's?"

A moment later, I heard the rustling of one of the bags, and then one of the half-dozen dinners being un-wrapped. "Mummmmph, I was beginning to think I might waste away," he said, not really joking, and then taking another big bite.

As I pulled away from the curb, the Lancer had a decided lean to the left, and the engine seemed to growl a bit more than usual.

"I think you'll be okay," I said as we slowly gained speed, then watched in the rearview mirror as he bit into the second double cheeseburger. "We've got a pretty easy gig, Luscious. I'm just making sure no one bothers these folks. It's a house in a swanky suburban neighborhood, deck out the back, big yard. I had two incidents over the last three nights, cracked one guy over the head, the other ran away."

"What's so important the dudes are breaking in?" he asked, then crammed the remainder of the double cheeseburger into his mouth.

I went on to give Luscious a general explanation. I told him about Iggy and Iggy's peculiar lifestyle. I mentioned the program Iggy and Bonnie had developed and how they were going to attempt to sell it to a big internet retailer. I told him the kids were gone. I didn't mention I'd been sleeping with Bonnie or that I'd gone and talked to Niles Wegger. I skipped telling him about my conversation with Iggy and how he'd bugged Niles Wegger's computer, or how Niles had somehow recorded Bonnie and me in the shower.

"Sounds like a laid back gig, well, as long as those dudes stay the hell away," he said, then took another large bite. He'd moved on to the big Macs by this point, taking a giant-sized bite out of one, chewing aggressively like he was under a major time constraint, then attacking the thing again. He'd devoured it in just over four bites, then grabbed a large Strawberry shake and sucked the entire thing down in about thirty seconds while taking a short break from chewing. By the time we pulled into Bonnie's driveway, he was finishing the apple pies and sucking down the last of the shakes.

"So here we are, man. Might as well go on in and get you situated."

The car rocked back and forth as Luscious slid across the backseat and eventually out the door. I think I heard the struts in the car gasp a sigh of relief once he was out and standing in the driveway. He stood there in the oil slick the Lancer had left, holding the last of a strawberry shake while cramming the remnants of a final apple pie into his mouth.

I noticed he'd undone his belt, or maybe he'd just forgotten to buckle it. Not that he could see that fact from his particular vantage point. Come to think of it, maybe he just couldn't buckle it. "Let's go on in," I said and unlocked the door. "Go ahead and make your way upstairs, Luscious. I'm just going to check on Iggy downstairs." I hurried down the lower set of stairs and knocked on the door as Luscious groaned with every step he took up to the main floor. The staircase groaned back.

I knocked again, this time calling Iggy's name. I was just starting to get worried when he answered.

"Who's there?"

"It's me, Iggy, Dev. Everything okay?"

"Yeah, yes," he said, sounding rushed. "I'm in the middle of a Linux update, so I have to go. Who was that big guy?"

"Friend of mine. His name is Luscious. He's going to help out over the next few days," I said, then wondered how he knew Luscious was big. All the windows in the lower level were covered. Maybe he heard the staircase groan? Then I remembered he'd taped Bonnie and me and that he'd installed visual access to the entire upper floor.

Twenty-three

onnie arrived home about an hour later. Luscious was stretched out on the living room couch, watching cartoons. He didn't move much, other than to wave a hand in the air when I introduced him. Morton was asleep on the floor in front of him.

"Nice to meet you," Bonnie said, not sounding all that sure, then looked at me like I was crazy. "I think I might need a glass of wine, want to join me on the deck?" she said, nodding toward the sliding door and using a tone that suggested I really didn't have another option.

I filled a glass with water, carried it out to the deck, and stood at the railing examining the backyard. Bonnie came out a few minutes later and closed the sliding door.

"That's the guy you got to help? What? You just gonna have him lay in front of the door, and anyone who tries to break in will have to climb over?"

"We've worked together before. He's low-key. Okay, very low-key, but he's good. Used to play for the NFL."

"The NFL, really?"

"Yeah, he was a tight end."

"I'm not even going to comment. Did you meet that Wegger character this morning?"

"I did, he offered me more money than I'd ever have a use for, which tells me we've been doing something right. It's why I brought Luscious here. I'm thinking in the next couple of nights something's going to happen. Iggy said you're flying out tomorrow?"

"Yeah. You talked with him, Iggy?"

"Yeah, we discussed bugging techniques. It was pretty much over my head, but we discussed it. Why?"

"Why? You've seen his paranoia in action, the tinfoil, the lights off, about a thousand different levels of security on the computers. As far as I knew, I was the only one the poor guy's ever talked to, and suddenly he's chatting with you? I mean, don't get me wrong, I think it's great, really I do. I just find it, I don't know, amazing."

"Hey, I'm a caring, sensitive kind of guy. Who wouldn't want to get to know me?"

"Yeah, right," she said and took a sip of wine. "Let's talk about my trip for a moment. I plan to fly to Seattle tomorrow. If everything goes okay, I should get in around four. I have a nine o'clock meeting the following morning. I expect to be home tomorrow evening, unless."

"Unless?"

"Unless everything goes according to my hopes and dreams, and I'm suddenly whisked in to meet Jeff Bezos."

"Who?"

"Ahhh, Dev! Where have you been the last twenty-plus years? Jeffrey Preston Bezos, born January twelfth, 1964. Founder and CEO of Amazon. If that guy wants to meet me, I'm there, no matter what it takes."

"I wish you luck. I mean it. Wouldn't that be cool if he wanted to see the product, and you had to stay over?"

"Yeah, thanks."

"How are you planning to get to the airport?"

"I was gonna call a cab."

"How about I give you a ride? I'd feel better knowing you got there safely, just for starters. Besides, with Luscious here, Iggy won't be alone, and I'll leave Morton, just to be sure." Bonnie gave me a look like she wasn't all that impressed.

* * *

She was up at six the following morning. Her flight left at two, but now, due to the improvements with TSA and the new security features, a three-hour, rather than two-hour lead time was recommended at the Minneapolis/St. Paul airport. It had gotten so bad that the head of the TSA had paid a visit, then, at no surprise, declared everything to be working splendidly. Our government at work.

I let Iggy know I was driving Bonnie to the airport, although, since she and I had talked about it in bed last night, I'm sure he already knew. I put Luscious in charge of security and Morton in charge of Luscious.

Our drive to the airport was uneventful. I kept my eyes on the road while Bonnie reviewed pages of notes. I parked the car at the airport rather than just drop her off at the curb.

"Dev, it's really not necessary. The Delta counter is about ten feet on the other side of the door."

"Yeah, I know, but just to be on the safe side. Depending on how desperate Wegger is, I want to see you get through security and be at least somewhat safe on the other side."

"How very sweet and totally unnecessary," she said, then went back to her notes.

If there was someone following, I never spotted them. She checked in at the kiosk, printed off a boarding pass, then wound her way through the forty-minute line to get through security. I stayed with her the entire time, looking around, and never spotted anyone even remotely suspicious other than a bald guy arguing with the TSA woman because he wanted to bring an expensive bottle of whiskey in his carry-on luggage. He ended up furious, red-faced, and whiskey-less, grumbling and swearing as he passed through the scanner. The TSA crowd couldn't seem to wipe the smiles off their faces.

From the airport, I made a quick stop at the office just to check the mail.

"Oh, you out already?" Louie asked, looking up from his computer.

"What are you talking about?"

"The cops, they didn't find you? They were here yesterday afternoon and again about two hours ago."

"Cops?"

"Yeah, two plainclothes guys. I have to say, not much of a sense of humor. Left their cards on that stack of mail on your desk."

"What'd they want?"

"They wouldn't say. I even told them I was your attorney. But all they did was smile. At least I think it was a smile."

"Cops?"

"Yeah, cards say Major Crimes Division, Vice. Maybe a one-nighter you forgot to pay?"

"Very funny," I said and sat down at my desk. I tossed the two business cards off to the side, then went through my mail, such as it was. I had a half-dozen grocery store circulars, two offers for cable TV, four or five credit card offers, and a letter from my bank with a five-hundred-dollar returned check written to me from a client. The check was stamped 'ACCOUNT CLOSED.' Perfect.

"Hey, look. I think those are the same two guys that were here earlier this morning," Louie suddenly said. He was leaning back in his office chair, casually gazing out the window.

I picked up the binoculars I use to watch the girls in the third-floor apartment across the street. I didn't recognize either guy stepping out of the car, but if you knew they were cops and then saw them, you'd say, "Oh yeah."

Both were in sport coats, no ties, one had jeans, the other wore what looked like khaki slacks. They had to wait for a moment while a bus, and a couple of cars passed before they crossed the street. Their car was a dark blue Ford Escort. Through the binoculars, I could just make out the flashing lights setup positioned low in the rear window. As they crossed the street, the cop in jeans pointed to my Lancer and said something to his partner. The partner nodded, and the two of them seemed to pick up their pace.

"I'm out of here, Louie. See if you can get them to step inside and close the door."

"You don't want to talk to them?" he called as I hurried out the door and down the hall. A moment later, I heard the door to the building open and then footsteps on the stairs just as I pushed open the door to the ladies' room.

I waited behind the door and counted to sixty, hoping they couldn't hear my heart pounding from down the hall. Once I finished counting, I cautiously opened the door and peeked out. God bless Louie, the office door was closed.

I hurried down the stairs, quietly opened and closed the door to the building, and then hugged the front of the building until I was just opposite my car. I had my car keys in my hand, ran to the driver's door, slid behind the wheel, and prayed the beast would start. It did, thank

God. I took a quick right at the corner, another right at the next, and then drove down the block and parked on the side street. Even if they saw me take off, there was less than a slim chance they'd follow the route I'd taken. I waited a couple of minutes, didn't see the dark blue Escort, and quickly drove over to my place.

As I drew closer to my place, I noticed a squad car parked across the street from the house. Two guys were sitting in the front seat, involved in an animated conversation of some sort. I just kept on driving, got on the interstate, and headed toward Bonnie's.

Twenty-four

I pulled into Bonnie's driveway and parked next to her car. I entered the garage through the side door and pressed the button to raise the garage door. I had to move a large plastic castle, two snow sleds, a wagon, a couple of bikes, a set of Hot Wheels, a doll buggy and a five-gallon bucket full of Legos before I'd cleared a space large enough to park. I pulled the Lancer into the garage, then lowered the door. I went into the house through the front door. Morton and Luscious remained asleep on the couch. An empty ice cream container with a spoon resting in the bottom sat on the coffee table. A plate that looked to have been licked clean and a fork lay next to Morton. An empty box of Hungry Jack pancake batter and an empty bottle of maple syrup sat on the kitchen counter next to the stove with the frying pan. Apparently, Luscious had made the two of them a small snack of a couple dozen pancakes.

I checked the backyard just because, made sure the board was still in position behind the sliding door, then ran downstairs and knocked on Iggy's door. He responded after the third set of knocks.

"Yes?"

"Iggy, it's Dev. Can we talk?"

The door opened a moment later, and I stepped in.

"Problems, I'm guessing," he said, then pulled the Mylar sheet just that much tighter around his shoulders and up over the back of his tinfoil hat.

"You're telling me," I said, stepping into the darkness. I waited for him to close the door and made a mental note of the fact that at least he gave me enough time to enter the room.

"So tell me," he said, heading for a chair once he closed the door.

I told him about the police looking for me, handed their business cards over to him, then told him about the squad car parked across the street from my house and how I just drove past and out here to Bonnie's.

"And you're sure they didn't follow you?"

"I checked at least a half-dozen times. Took some strange turns, circled back, but thankfully never saw anything. When I got here, I cleared a space in the garage and pulled my car inside."

"Did you check it for a tracking device?"

"A tracking device?"

"You know, the kind that attaches magnetically. It would most likely be around one of the bumpers, maybe in the wheel well or attached to the engine. Better go check now, just to be sure."

"We watched them get out of their car. They hurried across the street and into the building, never stopped for a moment."

"True, but weren't you parked at the airport for an hour, maybe longer?"

I thought about that. "I'll be back in a minute." I hurried out to the garage, got down on my hands and knees, and gave the Lancer a thorough going over. There, just below the front bumper, was a small black unit. About the size of a small magnetic box you'd maybe keep a spare key in. I had to pull it off using some force. I went into the house, grabbed Bonnie's car keys then drove her car over toward the shopping mall, where I planned to attach the box to another vehicle. Halfway to the mall, I had to wait at a train crossing. Oil cars, and lots of them, moving slowly due to a curve before they headed for the straighter line that ran along the Mississippi, all the way down to the Gulf of Mexico. I was only the second car in line, so I climbed out, took the box, and walked to the tracks. Everyone sitting in cars seemed to be watching, no doubt wondering what I was going to do.

I attached the box to a slow-moving oil car and walked back to the car. I waited what seemed like another ten minutes before the crossing guards went up, then turned around in the first parking lot I came to and headed back toward Bonnie's.

"You found something?" Iggy asked when he opened the door.

"Yeah, I'm not sure how long it's been there. But it's gone now," I said then proceeded to explain. Even in the darkness, I thought I detected a smile flash across his face when I told him about attaching the device to the oil car. "I might have another problem."

"Oh?" he said, sitting down in front of the computers where I'd first met him.

"Yeah, I mentioned the two police officers who stopped at my office looking for me this morning, plainclothes, I'm guessing detectives. They were driving an unmarked car. While I was there, they returned, and I had to sneak out of the building. I told you I drove past my house, and there was a squad car parked across the street. I'm guessing they were there waiting to see if I might show up."

"Did you talk to them?"

"No, I just kept on going and came out here."

"And you don't know why they were looking for you?"

"No. They left their cards the first time. They're with the Major Crimes Division, Vice."

Iggy seemed to think for a moment. "Is your computer here?"

"No, it's at my office and…"

My cellphone suddenly rang, Louie. "Here's my office mate. Let me take this. I'll get an update. Louie, you okay?"

"Yeah, I'll send you my bill later. Hey, those cops are not too happy with the fact that you weren't here. They saw your car out front when they came in."

"What did they want?"

"Not exactly sure, they were going to tow your car, but obviously that didn't work. They had a warrant for your computer. Thankfully, I wasn't mentioned in the warrant, but I have a feeling they could be back to grab mine. I might be working out of that back room at The Spot for the next few days.”

“They took my computer?” I said and looked over at Iggy. He nodded, then rolled his chair in the opposite direction and fired up two more computers.

“Yeah, didn’t say much more, other than to try and convince me the warrant covered everything in the office. They ran into a wall on that one,” Louie chuckled.

“Okay. Sorry for the hassle, Louie.”

“Not a problem, I’m packing up and heading to The Spot right now. I’ll probably be over there until I hear different from you.”

“Sorry, man,” I said again.

“Like I said, you’ll get my bill.”

“The police confiscated your computer?” Iggy said as I ended the call.

“Yeah, apparently they showed up with a warrant for the thing, and he had to let them take it. He’s my attorney,” I added, hoping that might add some credibility to the situation.

“We’ve probably got some time, but not much. Is your computer password-protected?”

“Maybe.”

“I’m not sure I’m following.”

“Well, you need the password to open it, but I have that always displayed, so right now, when you just click the start button, it comes on, and you’ve kind of got access to everything.”

"What kind of a system is it?"

"System?"

Iggy took a deep breath and exhaled. "You don't know what OS you have?"

"OS?"

"Operating System."

"Not really."

"Do you know the manufacturer?

"It has an HP on the front."

"And how long have you had it?"

"God, let me think." I couldn't really remember the year I'd purchased the thing, so I was counting back in girlfriends, Angie, Lisa, Mary Lou, Mai, Lisa again, AJ, Molly, Pattie, Rae Lynn, Carol, a couple of weekend get-aways I was drawing a blank on, Heidi intermixed off and on with all of them.

"How long?" Iggy asked again.

"I'm working on it. Maybe eight, nine years. This girl I was dating sent me a couple of selfies she took when we went to Las Vegas. She got bored with watching the Super Bowl in our hotel room. The Giants beat the Patriots that year. I remember that. Well, and the selfies she sent from the bathroom to get me away from the game."

Iggy was clicking keys as he asked, "Was your computer new when you purchased it?"

"Yeah, I got it for Christmas that year, a little gift to myself. Business expense," I laughed.

Iggy didn't seem too impressed. "Figure October, November of 2007. Good, Linux, Windows XP," he said. He clicked some more keys then muttered, "Mobile five, I A thirty-two, X Sixty-four. What is your email address?"

I told him.

"And the password?"

"One-two-three-four-five, easy to remember and lots of numbers," I said, thinking that might suggest I wasn't a lightweight when it came to security.

He stopped typing for a moment and looked at me, "You're kidding. That's the most popular password for the past few years running. Good lord, it's probably the first thing any amateur hacker would try."

"Oh," I said and couldn't think of anything else.

"Okay, now this, great, think we've got it. Yes, does this look familiar?" he said a few moments later, then turned the screen in my direction. The screen was exactly what my computer displayed when I turned it on. The image of Rae Lynn, a woman I used to date with her bikini top slung over her shoulder. The way the shot was taken, it didn't expose her, well, except for the bare shoulder, more's the pity, I always thought, she'd been very blessed.

"Anything you're aware of that might cause a problem, threats against the President, attempts at stealing funds from someone's account, some other fraudulent enterprise, maybe an internet scam, anything along those lines?"

"No, not really. As you may have guessed, I'm not really a computer guy."

"And you said the officers were from the vice squad?"

"That's what their cards said."

"Let's check your images," he said, clicking keys. It took about a minute, before he pulled up a file labeled Party-Time.

"What the hell? That's not mine. I've never seen that thing before."

He clicked on the file, and an initial image popped up. It looked like a wheel of some sort with a bunch of puzzle pieces. He clicked more keys over the course of a couple of minutes, and suddenly, the thing swirled into a legible image of a small child, a little girl. She couldn't have been more than five or six years old, and she was naked. Iggy glanced over at me.

I spoke before he had a chance to say anything. "Believe me, I've never seen that picture. I'll kill whoever loaded that on my computer."

"According to the file, there are over a thousand images. This is probably one of the more tame ones."

"Jesus, delete that shit."

"We'll do better than that. A simple delete will still leave a trail on your computer. I think we'll reinstall this on one of Niles Wegger's devices, one he won't suspect."

"You can get into his computers?"

"I told you before, I already have. I'm going to go through your files, all of them, just to be on the safe side, make sure there aren't more plants like this."

"That could take forever."

"I'll do it based on date added. It won't be that difficult, you've only been involved for what, a little more than seventy-two hours?"

"Yeah, something like that."

"I'll go back twice as long, just to be safe. But I'd better get on it. No telling how soon the police will access the computer. Do you have another system, one at your home?"

"No, just the one laptop. I've got cable and Netflix at home."

He gave me a quick look then said, "You should be okay, but let me get working on this now. I'll start with a new password and some added security, that will buy us more time," he said, then turned back to the computer screen and began clicking keys a mile a minute.

"Thanks, Iggy, you're a lifesaver. I'll let myself out." He gave a quick wave with a latex-gloved hand and nodded but didn't say anything.

Twenty-five

I phoned Louie back from out on the deck. Luscious and Morton, my security team, were both snoring. "Hi, Louie, it's Dev," I said once he answered. "Man, Iggy, this computer guy, accessed my laptop. Someone loaded a bunch of kiddie porn on there. He found a file with a thousand images."

"You gotta be kidding."

"I wish, he's going to erase them or delete them or something. Bastards had access to my computer."

"You mean someone broke into the office?"

"Not exactly, apparently my password was a little lax."

"There's a surprise."

"He's gonna fix that, too. Anything else with those two cops?"

"No, except they didn't want to believe you weren't here when they saw your car parked on the street. Then, when they finally did leave, and your car was gone, well, let's just say they weren't too happy. I told you they were gonna have it towed."

"Yeah. I catch the bastard that put that shit on my laptop, I'll kill him."

"As your attorney, I have to caution you about…"

"You know what I mean. Cops were outside my house, too."

"The two detectives?"

"No, a squad car parked across the street. Plus, there was a tracking device on my car." I went on to tell Louie about pulling the device off my car and attaching it to the train. "I'm sure the cops have everyone on the lookout for my license plate, damn Lancer sticks out like a sore thumb as it is. I'm going to be driving Bonnie's Santa Fe for the next day or so. I'll have to figure something else out once she gets back in town."

"Good luck, man. Listen, I hate to cut you off, but I fully expect those guys to be back with a warrant to grab my computer and anything else they can think of. I need to get out of here. You want me, I'll be in that back room at The Spot. You think of coming back here to the office, check with me first, okay?"

"Yeah. Thanks, Louie," I said and hung up.

I knocked on Iggy's door and told him I was going grocery shopping.

"I think we're almost out of hot dogs," he said, followed by the sound of continual keys clicking on the keyboard.

"Hot dogs, got it. Anything else you need?"

"No."

I could tell we were establishing a relationship. One conversation where he basically suggested I was an idiot, and now this one covering hot dogs, lucky me.

I picked up the hot dogs, along with hot dog buns, two roast chickens, mashed potatoes, a new tub of ice cream, two boxes of Hungry Jack pancake batter, an apple pie, a gallon of milk and a bag of bite-size Butterfinger candy bars.

When I returned to Bonnie's, Morton was awake, although he hadn't moved. Luscious was still sound asleep. I placed the roast chickens and mashed potatoes in the oven and turned it onto the warm setting. Then boiled up a couple of hot dogs and brought them down to Iggy. I must have made a tiny bit of progress earlier because he actually opened the door and let me bring his hot dogs into his dark cave instead of just leaving them on the stairs.

"I've taken the liberty of rearranging your computer files with a view toward increased efficiency," he said, taking the plate of hot dogs from me. "I've also added some additional security and set a new password," he said, then laughed to himself.

"What's so funny?"

"Bit of humor on my part is all."

I could only imagine. "I'm always up for a joke, Iggy."

"Ahhh, well, yes, I'm sure you'll see the humor. How's this for your new password, ready? Securitas six-twelve," he said, then stood there in the dark and laughed out loud.

"What am I missing?"

"Oh, come on, don't you get it? The Latin root word for security, along with your birthdate, six-twelve, June twelfth. That is your birthday, isn't it?" he asked, suddenly sounding all concerned.

"Yeah, that's my birthday. Oh, sure, of course, the Latin root, what was I thinking?" I said, thinking I'd better write it down and keep it in my wallet. My previous password might not have been too secure by Iggy's standards, but at least I could remember the damn thing.

"There's an option for you to list three security questions, and I've added some additional levels beyond that. I'd recommend attaching a biometric scanner. They can be acquired for a modest investment. That, along with the levels I've added, should keep you relatively safe."

"A biometric scanner?"

Iggy stared at me for a long moment. I took comfort in the fact he didn't sigh this time. "Biometrics. For our purposes, matching a number of features in your fingerprint pattern."

"Oh, a fingerprint scanner."

"Yes, a *fingerprint scanner,*" he said, taking the low road.

"Great idea. I'll look into that."

"Please, I highly recommend it. Biometrics would eliminate a number of potential problems for you. Now, to that end, I went ahead and eliminated a number of files on your system. Of course, that dreadful file placed there."

"So, you found more files besides that one you opened?"

"Not in so many words. There were, how shall I say, a number of images in a variety of boudoir styles that left nothing to the imagination."

"Iggy, talk English to me, man. Where is this coming from?"

This time he did give an audible sigh, then looked down longingly at the plate of hot dogs he still held. "I'm referring to your collection of naked images apparently from a variety of different women. Many taken in a similar, if not the exact, same setting."

"My bedroom. You deleted all those? My collection? Please tell me I'm wrong."

"Better safe than sorry. A number of the women appeared to have been more than a little intoxicated. Does the name Bill Cosby have any connotation?"

"Hey, they weren't drugged, it's more like we were just party animals and one thing led to another."

"Not to worry, the images have been eliminated."

"Wonderful," I said, meaning anything but.

"I sent an anonymous email to the police department's tip line, then scheduled two others to be sent over the next thirty-six hours from different email addresses. I would think they'll be paying a call to our mutual friend Mr. Wegger in the very near future."

"Good, it'll serve him right."

That seemed to bring a smile to Iggy's face, "If there's nothing else," he said, then raised the plate of hot dogs.

"No, that's it for me, nothing else. Iggy, thanks for your help. I would have completely missed that file of images, and the cops would have locked me up, then thrown away the key until they sorted it out, and I can't say that I'd blame them."

Iggy smiled, hurried to the door and let me out. I went back upstairs to review my security team.

Luscious was awake, finally, but still in the same position on the couch. "Man, Dev," he said as I came up the stairs to the main floor. "Something smells awfully good in here. That wouldn't happen to be roast chicken, would it?"

"Very perceptive, Luscious. You hit the nail on the head. If you want to get yourself cleaned up, we'll eat in about five minutes. I'm just going to set the table."

Luscious slowly rose to a sitting position, then slowly rocked back and forth a few times until he'd built up enough momentum to stand. He groaned as he got to his feet.

"Tough day, Luscious?"

"Been a lot of work. I took Morton for a walk while you were gone."

"You did?"

"Yes, sir. I took him out to the deck, and then he ran around the backyard for about ten minutes."

"You were with him?"

"Yes, sir. Well, I mean, I stayed on the deck, but I watched him the whole time."

"No wonder you're tired," I said, but I'm not sure he got the joke. Instead, he just nodded like that made perfect sense, then headed for the bathroom.

Twenty-six

We had dinner. I filled Morton's food dish with dog food, which caused him to look disdainfully from Luscious to me. I put some mashed potatoes on my plate, then passed the bowl to Luscious, who emptied the bowl. I'd placed both roast chickens on a large platter. I cut the thigh and a drumstick from one of the birds then passed the platter to Luscious. He placed the untouched roast chicken onto his plate and dug in.

"Glad you were able to grab some sack time this afternoon, Luscious. I'm thinking we'll work in shifts tonight. One of us always awake just watching. With Bonnie in Seattle, time seems to be running out on these jerks. If they're going to try anything, I'm thinking it's going to be sooner rather than later."

Luscious nodded, then pulled a drumstick bone out of his mouth, it was clean, not a hint of meat on it. "Sounds good to me, however you want to schedule things is fine. I'm usually up a couple of times just to fix a little snack, so whatever works." He expertly cut the entire breast off one side of the chicken sitting on his plate and started in.

"Mmm, one other thing," he said, then crammed another forkful of chicken and mashed potatoes into his mouth. "Might make sense to have whichever one of us is sleeping to take one of the beds in a bedroom instead of the couch. That way, they do try something, we could be, you know, like in reserve or something. Maybe set it up so we could page one another on our cellphones, you know, to alert us."

"Great idea, Luscious. We'll set it up after dinner."

Luscious was more than halfway through the first chicken breast when he carved the remaining breast off the chicken and piled it on his plate. Then he emptied the dressing out of the bird, aggressively digging with a spoon so he wouldn't miss any before he started in again on the pile of food.

"Tell you what, why don't you take that first shift around eleven. I'll relieve you from, say, two to six in the morning. That sound okay?" I asked.

His mouth was too full to speak. So he simply pointed at his mouth and nodded in agreement.

"Once you're finished eating, go do whatever you want, just be back here by eleven. Okay?"

He nodded, chewed a little more before he took an audible swallow. "Oh, man, really good. Hey, you gonna eat any more?" His plate was still piled with food, and there was more meat remaining on the chicken resting on his plate.

"No, to tell you the truth, Luscious, I'd just be stuffing myself at this stage. You go on and dig in, help yourself."

That brought a smile to his face, and he dug in, shoveling food like he was already late catching a train. Once he finished the chicken breasts from his bird, he grabbed the remaining bird off the platter and set it on his plate. He set his silverware down, then picked up a bird in his hands and started gnawing away. I had trouble watching, and yet found it fascinating to see him in action. In less than fifteen minutes, he'd picked both birds clean, polished off six servings of mashed potatoes, and was rattling around in the empty bag of Butterfinger candy bars in the vain attempt to find one more.

"I might just run up to the store and pick up a few treats, you know, as long as I'm going to be up and working later tonight."

"Probably be a good idea," I said, then pulled a ten-dollar bill out of my pocket, handed it to him, and said, "Maybe grab a couple of bags, it could be a long night."

Twenty-seven

Luscious had finished the bag of Milky Ways before I went to bed at eleven. He woke me a half hour before my shift at two and said he was falling asleep. Morton just groaned and snuggled into the pillow. I watched Luscious stumble into what had to be J.D's room, heard the bed creak and groan as all four hundred pounds of fun climbed aboard. He was snoring two minutes later. I pulled the bedroom door closed, but it didn't seem to help. I could still hear him.

Amazingly, he'd forgotten four small Butterfinger candy bars on the kitchen counter. A dozen-and-a-half Milky Way wrappers were scattered around the couch area. I picked up the wrappers, tossed the empty cans of Coke in the recycling bin, and turned on the TV. Bonnie had something like a hundred and twenty cable channels available, but none of them offered anything I wanted to watch. Her Kindle sat next to the TV, so I turned it on and scanned through her library. It looked like a great selection if you were into romance. I wasn't.

I ended up choosing something entitled 'The Doctor Is In.' The cover featured a nurse with her white nurse's

uniform unbuttoned well below her waist and some naked guy with a six-pack stomach. You couldn't see his
face, and he was wearing a stethoscope around his neck.
It was billed as a medical mystery. The nurse, named
Gloria, was spanking him with a licorice stick and wor-
rying about some kid's flu symptoms on page one. I
didn't get any further. I went back to the cable channels,
flicked through all of the channels twice, and ended up
watching the morning news broadcast from the UK, a
six-hour time difference from where I was in Minnesota.
The news cycle was repeating itself by the time I got up
to use the bathroom. I turned the TV off, then walked
into the ensuite unit off Bonnie's bedroom. By now, I
was familiar enough with the house that I could find my
way in the dark. In case I had any doubts, Morton was
on the bed, snoring in time to Luscious' snores coming
from down the hall, the two of them acting like bedroom
fog horns.

While I was in the bathroom, I thought I might have
heard Luscious walking around, but that didn't seem to
make any sense. I turned the light off and poked my head
out the door. Morton was still snoring, but I couldn't hear
Luscious. I had just stepped into the hall when a shadow
sailed out of the room Luscious was in, bounced off the
hallway wall, then dropped to the floor. A second figure
took a quick step or two out of the room before a massive
arm grabbed him by the hair and violently yanked him
back in. Someone cried out in agony a moment later, and
then all was quiet.

I had my pistol out and headed down the hall. The guy who'd bounced off the wall was in a half sitting position and very still. I didn't recognize him, but one thing was sure, he wasn't Luscious. I pressed my back against the wall, then called out. "Luscious, you all right?"

"These boys interrupted my dream. I was just about to cut into a thick juicy steak, and they had to spoil it for me. I'm all right, Mister Dev, but I ain't happy." Another voice groaned immediately after that.

I reached into the room and flicked on the light. Luscious was sitting on the bed, in the process of unwrapping a small Butterfinger. He was in his underwear, possibly the largest pair of plaid boxers I'd ever had the misfortune of seeing. He smiled at me as I stepped into the room with my pistol. A pair of legs jutted out from beneath one of his massive thighs. I could just make out a head squirming from beneath his other thigh. The face was scarlet, heading toward purple, and looked to be in a good deal of pain.

"Luscious, I think you're killing that guy. It looks like he can't breathe, he's turning purple."

The guy attempted to groan, but he emitted just a short little squeak, not very loud, it sounded like air escaping from a balloon. I guessed he'd probably suffocate in the next sixty to ninety seconds if Luscious didn't get off him.

"Maybe you should let him up before he dies."

"It's not like we invited the two of them in, Dev. You know, enter at your own risk. Then they proceeded to threaten someone, namely me. All I was doing was just trying to get a decent night's sleep. I don't know."

I heard something out in the hallway and peeked out. The guy on the floor appeared to be coming around, gradually. At least he could move his head from side to side and give a little groan.

"I found a couple more of those candy bars. I left them out on the kitchen counter for you. If you're interested."

"Butterfingers?"

"Yeah, they're on the kitchen counter, right by the wastebasket, well, unless these guys took them."

Luscious' eyes went wide at the thought of someone eating his candy bars. "How many were left?"

"I think there were four. Maybe check to see if they're still there."

He nodded then slowly rose with a groan. The guy beneath him, now a dark purple, inhaled deeply, rolled off the bed, dropped to the floor and lay face down. Luscious stepped out of the room, and a moment later, I heard a cry. I popped my head into the hall again, and there was Luscious, grinding his foot with most of his weight behind it into the guy's hand. It might have been a carpeted hallway, but with Luscious grinding, I envisioned a number of broken bones.

Neither one of these idiots was in any condition to go anywhere. Luscious eventually stepped off the hand, and the guy immediately started crying and curled into a fetal position.

Luscious had left his cellphone on the bedside table, and I picked it up and called 911.

"Ramsey County emergency services."

"Yeah, hi, I just had a break-in at a home I'm watching for the owner. I've detained two individuals. Umm, they'll probably need an ambulance to take them to the hospital."

There was a slight pause before the dispatcher replied. "You have them detained?"

"Yeah, two of them. If you could send the police and probably the paramedics."

"What's the address?"

I gave her the address, then confirmed the phone number and gave her my name, Luscious Dixon. The guy on the bedroom floor was bleeding from his mouth, I guessed cracked or broken ribs, maybe a collapsed or punctured lung. The guy in the hallway was sobbing, more or less silently, still in the fetal position. I walked out to the kitchen where Luscious was running his finger across the kitchen counter to pick up the last bit of crumbs from the candy bars.

"Hey, Luscious, I called the cops, they'll be here in a couple of minutes. I'm going to step outside. You'll have to deal with them."

"What?"

"They're just going to arrest these two jerks. Paramedics will be here, too. Your friends are not in the best of shape."

Luscious just shrugged.

"I'm sure once they come with sirens on, a couple of folks will be outside, neighbors. I'll just stand out there, so I won't be far away. Think you can handle that?"

"You sure? You know how I don't like confrontation."

"Yeah, I'm aware of that, and yes, you can handle this. I doubt there will be any confrontation. Tell you what, maybe pull on some pants and then help yourself to the ice cream in the freezer. Caramel something or other with big chunks of chocolate in it. Okay?"

He seemed to consider that option for a moment, then nodded and headed down the hallway to the bedroom. He was back a minute or two later with his jeans at least on, if not buckled. He hadn't bothered with a shirt. I could hear a siren in the distance.

"Just tell them these guys broke into the house and threatened you. Here," I said, pointing at a whiteboard on the refrigerator door. "This is the contact information for Bonnie. They can call her if they need to. Like I said, I'll just be out front, but they were looking for me on another matter, and I don't need the hassle. Okay?"

Luscious looked like he was searching for something to say but finally nodded his head yes.

"Good, you grab a spoon while I get that ice cream out for you." I opened the freezer compartment and pulled out the plastic pail of ice cream. It was labeled as family size, a full gallon, and I had no doubt Luscious would finish it all by himself. "Appreciate you doing this favor for me," I said as the siren grew louder.

Luscious smiled. I wasn't sure if it was because of what I just said, or rather, the fact that I handed him a gallon pail of ice cream.

Twenty-eight

I cut through three backyards, walked between two houses, out onto the street, and then headed back toward Bonnie's. There was a squad car out in front of her place, and an ambulance was in the process of backing into the driveway next to her car. Maybe a half-dozen people were milling around out in front of the house, most wearing hastily thrown-on clothes, although one woman wore fuzzy white slippers and a blue terrycloth bathrobe. She glanced in my direction and eyed me suspiciously. I hung back by the street and asked some guy in shorts and a t-shirt what was going on.

"Not sure, I'm guessing probably a heart attack, something along those lines. Poor soul."

"Do you know the family?" I asked.

"No, no. Seen the kids once in a while, the mom, but never spoken to them."

Two of the paramedics walked back outside, opened up the rear doors of the ambulance, then pulled a gurney out of the back and rolled it up to the front door.

"Yeah, looking an awful lot like a heart attack," the guy next to me said. About ten minutes later, two police officers brought someone out in handcuffs. I recognized him as the guy from the hallway. He was limping, with an officer holding onto either arm. He held his hand out in front of him with a bandage wrapped around it. The arm was in a sling, and he looked like he was still crying. He scanned the crowd as they led him to the squad car. He seemed to do a quick double-take when he looked at me. I smiled back as the officers gently guided him into the rear seat of their squad car. Once they closed the door, the cops looked at one another, shook their heads, and laughed before they headed back into the house.

It was another ten minutes before the paramedics wheeled out the gurney with the other guy on it. He didn't look too hot, and he had an oxygen mask covering his face. One of the paramedics carried an IV drip bag and walked alongside the gurney. The ambulance left a few minutes later with flashing lights but no siren. The cops left five minutes after that. I lingered at the edge of the front yard until everyone had returned home. The woman in the blue bathrobe was the last one to leave, and she gave me a long look before departing.

As she walked back to her house, I slipped alongside Bonnie's garage, then made my way up the stairs to the deck and into the kitchen through the back entrance. Luscious was seated on the couch, watching cartoons and eating out of the ice cream pail. Two-thirds of the ice cream was already gone.

"Everything go okay?"

Luscious licked his spoon and nodded. "Yeah, they were really nice," he said, sounding more than a little surprised.

"They ask about me at all?"

"Nope. I'm going to have to file a report, but I can do it on a computer later today. They gave me a case number. I got it written down on one of those cards on the kitchen counter there."

"Those two guys ever talk or say anything?"

"The guy I sat on couldn't seem to talk. He just kept gasping and groaning. The other one never stopped crying, and he kept asking the cops to take him away. I guess they didn't like me very much."

"You did what you had to do, Luscious. Remember, they ruined your dream about that steak."

"Yeah, that's what I told the cops. They thought that was pretty funny."

"They ask anything about Bonnie?"

"No, I gave them her name, and they wrote down that phone number, but that's all. Guess what?"

"What?"

"One of the paramedics knew me."

"Knew you?"

"Well, about me, he told the bunch of 'em I was in the NFL, and then he asked me for my autograph. Pretty cool, huh?"

"That's really cool, Luscious. You save the day here, and those guys get to meet a hero. I'd say that's a pretty successful day, and the sun isn't even up yet."

Luscious smiled and dug deeper into the gallon pail of ice cream.

"Tell you what, Luscious, if you want to hit the sack, that's okay with me. I'm not going to be able to sleep, and I want to check in with Iggy, downstairs. They didn't go down there, did they?"

"No, never even asked about it. Once those two started whining and crying, well, they just got them out of here and told me thanks for helping out."

"Proud of you, Lucious. Well done."

Luscious smiled, then rocked back and forth until he had enough momentum to stand up from the couch. "Think I'll be going back to bed," he said, then headed down the hallway with what was left of the ice cream.

Twenty-nine

I had to knock on Iggy's door a number of times before he answered. "Who, who is it?"

"It's just me, Iggy, Dev." I heard what sounded like a sigh of relief, or was it a groan? I couldn't be sure. The door opened a moment later.

"You never responded to my messages."

"You sent me a message?"

"Text messages on your cellphone, three of them, as a matter of fact. I saw those two on the deck. The lock only took them a moment, and apparently, you hadn't bothered to place the board behind the door again." He turned and walked into the darkened room.

"Could you see them on your computers?"

"Yes, but like I said, the door off the deck only took them a moment. Once they were inside, I could barely make them out in the dark."

"Yeah, well, fortunately for us, they woke up Luscious."

"Yes, they thought he might be me. They called him by my name."

"They did?"

"Right before he attacked them. It happened so fast, and since the lights were off, I couldn't make out what had happened. Then you were there and turned on the lights."

"I would say they're getting desperate, especially with Bonnie's meeting scheduled for tomorrow. I wonder if they have anyone waiting for her out in Seattle."

"I've already sent her a warning. Told her we had yet another incident here," Iggy said. Even in the dark, I could tell he was staring at me and not at all pleased.

"That was their third attempt," I said. "Hopefully, they'll get the message this time. I'm sorry about all this, Iggy. I'm just glad you're okay."

"It could have been catastrophic. They could have bundled me off to God knows where or gained access to all my systems," he said, then glanced around at his computers like they were his children, which, in a way, I guess they were. "I can't sleep. I'm constantly monitoring. I send you alerts, warnings, information, and you don't seem to pay attention. I don't know…"

He sat there in the dark, feeling sorry for himself. For just a half-second, I wondered what possible series of situations growing up would cause someone to wrap themselves in Mylar and live in the dark. But that was unfair, he was probably the smartest kid in the class, and 'normal' idiot kids like me would have picked on him. Then add to that working for some government agency no one wanted to talk about, and it all started to make sense, I think.

"Iggy, I'm not going to let anyone get to you, I promise. And Luscious feels the same way. You're safe here. Luscious just put two guys in the hospital, and when they get out, they're going straight to jail. Wegger's days are numbered. You just keep on doing what you're doing, and we'll be one step ahead of him. He's getting desperate, that's why he's doing this crazy stuff. Okay?"

"Promise me you'll pay attention to the warnings I send."

"I promise. Is there anything else I can do to make you feel more secure?"

He thought about that for a moment, then said, "Your dog."

"Morton?"

"Yes. Maybe he could come to visit every once in a while."

"I'm not sure how he'll do in the dark, but let's try it. I'll go get him now."

"No, wait until he wakes up, had his breakfast, and his trip outside to do his duty."

"Okay, after breakfast, then."

"I'll download Dog TV for him."

"Dog TV?"

Iggy gave an exasperated sigh. "It's cable, for dogs. Highly effective in showing them proper play behavior and social interaction."

"Dog TV."

"Just have him down here later this morning, I'm already looking forward to the visit, and it will serve as a good diversion."

"Dog TV?"

Thirty

I could hear Luscious snoring from down the hall. Morton was sound asleep in bed, snoring. I checked my cellphone on the bedside table. I had three messages, all from Iggy, although at some point, I had apparently set my phone on silent. He was right to be upset. I phoned Bonnie a little after nine, Seattle was two hours behind us.

"Hello," she sounded wide awake.

"Hi, Bonnie, Dev."

"So, what's the word? I got a half-dozen messages from Iggy. The last one said things had quieted down. Thanks for talking to him, he can be wound a little tight from time to time."

"Gee, really? Luscious has to fill out some police form online later today. One, if not both of the intruders, are in the hospital. No damage done here. Like you mentioned, Iggy has more or less calmed down."

"One of his emails, I think the third or fourth, gave me the access code to his file with his last will and testament."

"That may have been a bit of an overreaction. Then again, he's seeing all this on his computer screens, living down there in the dark. Is it any wonder?"

"Yeah, and don't forget, at the end of the day, it was a break-in. That's terrifying for anyone."

"Things quiet out there?" I asked, Morton had just strolled past the kitchen and stood waiting by the sliding door.

"Yes, not a bother, but then again, they probably want me to succeed, so I'm not really anticipating any difficulty here. Just stay on top of things back there," Bonnie said.

I kept talking as I opened the sliding door and let Morton out. "Maybe the third time is the charm. First Wayne, then Wegger's younger brother, followed by these two fools early this morning, you'd think sooner or later someone would start to catch on."

"I'd say look for a change in tactics. I just wish we knew what it was going to be."

"Well, you just focus on your meeting this morning. Everything is fine back here. Let me know if you're flying home tonight. I'll pick you up at the airport."

"That would be nice, but you don't have to do it. I can just grab a taxi."

"Call me, and good luck later this morning."

I thought some more about where Bonnie was vulnerable. She was probably correct in her assessment that nothing was going to interfere with her meeting in Seattle. Success on that front was, after all, what all parties wanted. It would serve no purpose to destroy Iggy's computer systems or burn the house down. They'd tried to get me out of the way, and Luscious had thwarted that attempt. I couldn't think of anything else that could be eliminated or used as leverage. The kids were— the kids.

I kept thinking about the kids while Morton ate his breakfast. When he finished, I brought him downstairs to Iggy's and knocked on the door.

"Who's there?" Iggy asked a minute later.

"Hi, Iggy, it's Dev. Hey, I brought Morton down, if you've got time."

The door opened almost immediately, and as soon as it did, Morton began wagging his tail and banging it off the wall.

Iggy bent down and stuck his latex-gloved hand out from underneath the sheet of Mylar wrapped around his shoulders.

Morton hesitated for just a fraction of a second, then let Iggy scratch his head, which set Morton's tail going even faster.

"I'd say he likes you, Iggy."

"Then please come in, Morton," Iggy said and stepped out of the doorway. Light spilled out of the normally dark cave I'd gotten used to Iggy inhabiting.

"Iggy, you have lights?"

"Special low ambient light. It's what I usually have on when I work."

"But it's always been so dark when I've been in there. I thought you were working in the dark all the time."

"I just turn it off when someone's at the door. You never know who it could be, the darkness provides just that much more security, and, well, it shortens everyone's visits, too."

That actually made sense in a strangely peculiar, anti-social way. "Let me ask you something. I'm trying to get ahead of our friend Mr. Wegger. Bonnie's children are at her sister's in Wisconsin."

"Actually, I believe her sister lives here in town. She has the children at her lake place. It's Chrissy, right?"

"Yeah. Are you in contact up there? Happen to have the place monitored?"

"No, not at all. Why? Has something happened?"

"No, I'm not aware of anything. I'm just trying to think ahead. Wondering what the next move will be. I'm fairly sure there will be one, and it would be nice to know what it is sooner rather than later."

Iggy actually shook his head, suggesting I might be making sense. "Let me review the office recordings I've gathered. If I come across anything, I'll let you know. Would it be all right if Morton remained?"

"He can stay for as long as you'd like. I'll just be upstairs, page me," I said, then pulled the cellphone from my pocket and waved it at him.

He flashed the briefest of smiles and said, "That would be nice." Then he stepped inside and closed the door behind the two of them.

Thirty-one

At no surprise, Luscious was up in time for lunch. I'd just brought some hot dogs and Morton's bowl of dog food down to Iggy, and when I went back upstairs, Luscious was seated at the dining room table. "What's for lunch?" he asked.

I opened the refrigerator and took out a loaf of bread, then opened a kitchen cabinet and hauled out a jar of peanut butter and a jar of grape jelly. I placed the jars in front of Luscious and said, "Help yourself."

He didn't so much as blink, just opened the loaf of bread, and started making open-faced peanut butter and jelly sandwiches. He carefully spread the peanut butter across the slice of bread, making sure none of the bread showed, spreading the peanut butter right up to the edge of the crust. Then he did the same with the jelly, ate the piece in just three or four bites, and made the next one. He carefully licked the knife when he'd finished applying the peanut butter so as not to get any in the jelly jar and vice-versa, licking the jelly off the knife before inserting it into the peanut butter.

"How about some fruit for dessert? There's some nice apples over on the counter, and Bonnie has some oranges in the fridge."

"No, thanks," he said, then got up and stood in front of the refrigerator with the door open, scanning what was available on the shelves. He closed the door and gave a disappointed sigh.

"You finish that ice cream?"

"Yeah, just before I went to sleep."

"Tell you what, how about I draw up a grocery list, give you some cash, and you can do the shopping. Fair enough?"

"At the grocery store?"

"I've found that's one of the best places to get groceries."

"Yeah, I could do that. I was thinking I might go home and use my computer to file that police report online, too."

"Iggy offered to help."

"No offense, but the man really weirds me out."

"Yeah, although he's pretty nice once you get to know him. Morton's down there with him right now."

"He let Morton into that dark cave where he lives?"

"Yeah, they got along famously, and guess what else I learned?"

"What?"

"He's got lights on once the visitors leave."

"No shit?"

"I'm not kidding. The lights are on down there right now."

"That makes me feel a little better about the guy, but I'm still not going down there. If it's all right, I'd like to fill out that report from home."

"Fine with me, anything that will help get those two guys locked up. Breaking and entering, assault, they'll hopefully each draw a year and, with any luck, a very stiff fine."

"I'd just like to get my hands on them again."

"Believe me, Luscious, the last thing either one of those two want is to run into you again."

I drew up a grocery list, Luscious added a number of additional items, then left in Bonnie's car. I went downstairs and listened at Iggy's door. All I could hear was barking that must have been coming from the Dog TV channel, Morton was probably in his glory. My cell rang a little after three. A number that looked familiar, although I didn't recognize it right off the bat.

"Hello."

"Hi, Dev, just checking in to see if you're okay."

Angie, surprise, surprise. "How very nice of you to call, Angie." Her words from a while back about 'a little more stable and a lot more permanent' rang in my ear. "What can I do for you?"

"Just wanted to see how you're doing, is all."

I wasn't sure. She could have been dumped by whoever the guy was, but on the other hand, she was genuinely nice enough that maybe she really did call just to see if I was okay. "That's really nice, but not to worry. I've been really busy with work lately. In fact, I'm working now."

"Oh, is it a bad time, you want me to call back later?"

"Actually, would you mind if I called you? I'm working round the clock and pretty much on a short leash at the moment. Could I maybe give you a call in about a week?"

"A week?"

"Yeah, hopefully, I'll be finished with this case by that time."

"Yeah, sure, call when you can, glad you're busy."

"Thanks, Angie, really appreciate the call, I mean it. I'll talk to you later." My phone rang almost the moment I disconnected with Angie. "Hello."

"Hi, Dev, Bonnie. Everything okay back there?"

"Yes, in fact, it's wonderfully boring. More importantly, how are things going for you?"

"Well, I'm staying another night, keep your fingers crossed. I'll be meeting with more people tomorrow morning."

"That's great, so they were at least interested enough to have you back."

"Oh, yeah, actually I just got out of there, they took me to lunch, and I met a number of folks. They could not have treated me better. I'm just so excited. I felt like I had to tell someone."

"Really happy for you, want me to pass the information on to Iggy?"

"Oh, I already sent him an in-depth message. He's got all the facts and figures. How's he doing by the way? Have you seen him?"

"Actually, I think he's doing pretty well. He's had Morton down there for the better part of the day."

"Morton?"

"They seem to be getting along famously. Get this, he's got some dog TV channel running on one of his computers, and guess what else?"

"I give up?"

"He has lights on."

"You're kidding."

"No. Some low ambient things, but it's lit up in there enough that you can actually see who you're talking to."

"He didn't happen to lose the Mylar, did he?"

"Ahh, no, that was still tightly wrapped around him."

"One thing at a time, I guess. Oh, call coming through, maybe another appointment for tomorrow. Wish me luck," she said, then hung up before I could say goodbye.

Thirty-two

"I don't know, Dev. Like I just said, I waited until it was all clear, then put the blinker on, turned, and they came out of nowhere."

We were standing in the driveway looking at Bonnie's car, or what was left of it. The passenger side was all scraped and dented with a large orange streak running from the rear wheel up to where the headlight used to be.

"They didn't honk or anything? How fast were they going?" I felt like I was grasping at straws. Once you pull in front of a school bus, you're basically screwed. I knew for a fact, Luscious wasn't the best driver out there. Come to think of it, the last time I'd seen him drive, he ran into a median that 'Just popped up out of nowhere' and damaged a car while in the process of trying to hold onto a McDonald's shake, which got me thinking for a moment. "Did you spill the food?"

"Lost the shake on the floor, and the double cheeseburger went out the window. By the time I got out of the car, someone else had run over my cheeseburger, and there was nothing left to save."

Luscious, for want of a burger and a shake, thirty minutes after polishing off an entire loaf of bread along with a jar of peanut butter and another of jelly, had just done about five grand worth of damage to Bonnie's Santa Fe. And I was going to have to pay for the privilege. I peeked in the passenger window. Sure enough, it looked like strawberry shake slathered all over the carpet. Screaming wasn't going to help.

At that point, a car came down the street, then slowed to a crawl. With the tinted windows, I couldn't tell who was behind the wheel, but whoever was driving leaned toward the passenger window and examined the damage. The car resumed speed for two more houses, then pulled into the driveway and parked. The woman who wore the blue bathrobe the other night climbed out of the car, gave us a disdainful look, and went in her front door. A moment later, I caught a lace curtain moving on one of her front windows. I felt like giving her the finger but figured that would do nothing to help, so I just ignored her.

I helped Luscious carry six bags of groceries inside. Not bad, considering he was just going to pick up a couple of items. One of the bags had a large wet spot on the bottom. As soon as he saw it, Luscious cried, "The ice cream is melting." Then he sat down on the couch with the container and a spoon and went to work. I put the groceries away, then headed downstairs to check on Iggy and Morton.

The door was closed but not locked, which I found interesting. Iggy answered almost immediately. He still had his sheet of Mylar wrapped around him and the tin-foil cap, but the latex gloves were gone. The low ambient lights were still on in the room, giving everything a dusky cast which seemed preferable to the almost impenetrable darkness I'd seen up till now. I noted that when he opened the door, I didn't hear the lock snap, which meant he'd either forgotten to lock it or it was unlocked on purpose. Either way, I took it to be positive.

"Oh, hi, we were just watching the news," Iggy said, walking back to a chair.

The two of them had moved from the computer Iggy had originally turned on, to watching a large flatscreen, at least four feet long with a split image, one image seemed to be a continual news feed guaranteed not to help Iggy's neurosis, the other half looked like the dog channel. Morton lay on the floor, mesmerized.

"Just checking, everything going okay, Iggy?"

"Just fine, thank you. I got this flat screen from Amazon, same day delivery." He pulled the Mylar a little tighter around his shoulders, rested his chin on his chest, and looked over the top of his eyeglasses at the flatscreen.

I didn't want to ask what the cost was. Gee, imagine if I didn't have to pay for the car damage, maybe I could order one, too. "I spoke with Bonnie, she's been asked to meet again tomorrow, so she's going to spend another night in Seattle."

"Yes, she was kind enough to send a full report. Things seem to have gone rather well today."

"Congratulations to the two of you."

"Thank you," Iggy said, continuing to stare at the flatscreen.

"Okay, tell you what, I'm going to be upstairs. You just call or send Morton out whenever you've had your fill. You're sure he's not a problem."

"We're getting along fine. Thank you," he said, then indicated the door with a nod of his head.

Morton wandered upstairs just about dinnertime. Luscious and I had just sat down to a large meatloaf. I took a slice, Luscious took the rest. We decided to keep watch in shifts again, just to be on the safe side. Mercifully, nothing happened, and we sat down to a pancake breakfast bright and early at ten the following morning. The rest of the day was uneventful until Bonnie called from the Seattle airport just before dinnertime. She said she'd be home around ten and tell us all about her day once she arrived.

I picked her up from the airport and drove her home. She didn't seem that upset about the damage to her car. As a matter of fact, she didn't seem to be upset at all, passing the whole thing off with a shoulder shrug and an "Oh well, accidents happen."

I wondered what medication she was on but didn't pursue the matter since it seemed to be going my way. She flitted into the house and down to Iggy's level while I dragged her suitcase into the bedroom. I went to bed at half-past twelve. Bonnie was still downstairs talking to Iggy. I couldn't remember when she came to bed, only that she was there in the morning. So was Morton, taking up most of the middle of the bed, pushing me almost over the edge until it was just better for everyone if I got up and out.

Thirty-three

I brought breakfast hot dogs down to Iggy, along with Morton, once he'd been fed and had a chance to run around the back yard. Luscious had watched him from the deck while devouring a bag of Malted Milk Balls, so I could cook breakfast. I made three omelets, one for Luscious, one for Bonnie, and one for myself. Luscious finished his in record time, then stepped up to the stove where he made and ate a dozen large pancakes.

He'd pour one almost the size of the frying pan, then eat it while the next one was cooking. He occasionally took a long drink directly from the bottle of maple syrup like it was whiskey. Bonnie watched him, speechless, staring while he devoured three or four pancakes in that manner. She finally pushed back in her chair and said, "I have a ton of notes to go over with Iggy, and they'd like me back out in Seattle in forty-eight hours. I'll be down in the darkroom." She rolled her eyes, flashed a fake smile, then shook her head as she carried a number of files downstairs.

I brought two more hot dogs down to Iggy for lunch. Morton was on the floor, apparently watching the Dog channel, while Iggy and Bonnie worked through all sorts of changes and adjustments to the computer programs. The lights were on, but he was still wrapped in Mylar and wore the tinfoil hat, although the latex gloves were nowhere to be seen. Bonnie waved off anything for lunch and just asked for iced tea.

When I brought the glass of tea down, the two of them were still clustered around a computer, and Iggy seemed to be explaining something about currency exchange rates to her. Suddenly, two of the computers on the far side of the room began flashing red and making an emergency alarm sound. Bonnie looked up, Iggy quickly rolled his desk chair over to the computers, spinning halfway round as he shot across the room, so he was in the perfect position to attack the keyboard, which he did. I stood there with a blank look on my face holding Bonnie's tea.

"What is it? What's wrong?"

"No idea yet. I set up an audio program so that when certain words are spoken, and specific tones are recorded, we receive a warning."

"What?"

"What it means is someone was upset, raised their voices, using Bonnie's name or my name along with some rather colorful language. It may be related to the failed intrusion the other evening. It may be because they've learned of Bonnie's success out in Seattle, and they've given up."

"You think that could be it?"

"That doesn't sound like the Wegger I knew some years back. Not the sort to admit defeat. My guess, they're going to try something extreme."

"Extreme? Can we get all this stuff out of here?" I asked, looking around the room and knowing what the answer would be.

"Let's call the police," Bonnie said.

Iggy just kept clicking keys, Morton barked once or twice at the new flatscreen. In the end, we decided not to do anything. The recording that had set off the alarm was someone swearing, most likely Wegger, mentioning Iggy and Bonnie by name coupled with a string of expletives. But it sounded like he was leaving the room just as he got going, so whatever the cause or proposed action was, we remained essentially in the dark.

"Maybe we just heard him throw in the towel," Bonnie said.

I doubted things would work out that easily. Luscious and I remained on guard throughout the course of the evening. Luscious slept on the couch for a few hours, but I was too worked up to relax. In the end, nothing happened, and the sun rose on a new day with my eyes burning from lack of sleep and Luscious driving to the grocery store for more eggs and pancake mix.

Bonnie and Iggy worked through the day. I threw four steaks on the grill for dinner. One for Bonnie, one for me, two twenty-two ounce steaks for Luscious, and a couple of hot dogs for Iggy.

After dinner, Bonnie went back down to Iggy's and worked until sometime past midnight. She was in bed when Luscious woke me to stand guard at two, but I had no recollection of her having come to bed. Her clock alarm went off just before six when Luscious relieved me. She was stepping out of the shower as I crawled into bed.

"Got an extra ten minutes?" I asked as she toweled off.

"Oh, I'm sorry, that's so sweet…I think. We have to get these corrections input and then tested before I fly back out to Seattle. How does a raincheck sound?"

"Right now, not all that thrilling."

She smiled and pulled an olive-drab t-shirt on over her head. Just in case I wasn't getting the message, the front of the t-shirt had a large red circle with a line through it.

"Do you have much more work to do?"

"Tons, but it's the testing that takes so long. Believe me, if this works, it will be worth it. They told me when I was out there, they were going to put this on the fast track. God, they weren't kidding."

I left breakfast on the stairs for her and Iggy after knocking on the door. I did the same with lunch.

Thirty-four

I returned to collect the lunch dishes just as Iggy's phone rang. Bonnie opened the door for me. The ringtone was actually a male voice, harsh, deep, and threatening, "You will suffer."

"Who the hell is that?" I said both lack of sleep and lack of Bonnie had done nothing to improve my patience.

"Oh, my God, it's Wegger. That's the ringtone I assigned him some years ago. I haven't spoken to him since, well, forever."

"Aren't you going to answer?" Bonnie asked.

"Answer that damn thing," I said, more than a little creeped out.

"Hello?" Iggy answered, not sounding all that sure. "Speaking. Who is this? Really? Niles, how long has it been?" What little color there was suddenly drained from Iggy's face. He looked at Bonnie and me, pointed to his cellphone, and mouthed "Wegger," as if we needed an explanation.

I rotated my hand in a circular motion, suggesting he keep the conversation moving. He nodded, then said, "To what do I owe the pleasure? I see. No. No, I didn't know that. Really? An invitation, at almost four in the morning. I must have slept through it. No, a number of security people. I'm not sure. I lost count days ago."

Bonnie looked at me and made the crazy sign, twirling her index finger next to her temple. I nodded in agreement.

"Yes, quite successful, now that you mention it," Iggy said. "Well, yes, as a matter of fact, she is," he said and gave a worried look toward Bonnie. "Well, actually, we're both working just now, Niles. I'm sure you can understand, we've a lot to—" Iggy suddenly yanked the phone away from his ear and cringed. We could hear a voice screaming on the other end.

"He said he wants to talk to you," Iggy said, then handed the phone to Bonnie.

"Hello. Yes, this is Bonnie. I'm not sure I understand." The color suddenly drained from Bonnie's face, and her eyes grew wide. "J.D., is that you? Honey, are you all right?" Tears began rolling down her face. She nodded a few times but seemed unable to speak. I looked at Iggy, but he just stared at the floor. Bonnie gave a cry and then handed the phone to me.

"Hello."

"Is this that intrepid security agent, Devlin Haskell?"

"What can I do for you, Mr. Wegger?"

"What can you do for me? I think it's more like what I can do for you. Hold on, just a minute, I want you to talk to someone."

A moment later, a child's voice came across. "Hello?"

"I bet this is J.D., is that right?"

"Yeah, are you the guy with that dog that liked to catch the frisbee?"

Bonnie had both hands to her face, her eyes were squeezed closed, and tears were running down her cheeks. Iggy had rolled across the room in his chair and was madly tapping keys.

"Yeah, J.D., that's me. Are your brother and sister with you?"

"Yeah, we're all—"

Wegger was suddenly back on the line. "Now listen up, Haskell. I'm only going to say this once. It's actually a very simple request. I'm returning the children to their mother, after all, I'm not a criminal. In exchange for that, I would like access to Iggy's system for one hour, just sixty minutes. That's all."

"You bring the kids here, and it's all yours."

"I have a much better idea. Let's arrange access, oh, say, effective nine o'clock this evening. Once that's complete, you can pick them up. Fair enough?"

"I'll have to—"

"It was merely a rhetorical question, you idiot. Your job will be to convince your two employers there of the wisdom of complying with my request. I'm only going to ask once. Good day," he said and then hung up.

I handed the phone back to Bonnie, who snatched it from my hands, "J.D., J.D., honey. Are you there?"

"Wegger hung up," I said.

"I'm getting a location," Iggy said.

Thirty-five

"Anything on that location, Iggy?" He was still clicking keys, although now only occasionally. His cellphone was plugged into the computer. Bonnie was silently sobbing, with both arms wrapped tightly around her.

"What are you coming up with?" I'd taken up a position directly behind Iggy.

"They are, or at least were, in a vehicle, and I think moving."

"You mean you can't tell'?"

"Exactly. No doubt Wegger's pulled the battery on his cellphone, essentially halting my ability to track him any further."

"Any idea where they called from?"

"Someplace in north-central Wisconsin. I'm getting a lock on that transmission."

"Wisconsin? Bonnie, isn't that where your sister's lake place is?"

She looked up at me but didn't seem to quite comprehend.

"Bonnie, your sister's lake place, where the kids are, do you have the phone number?"

She shook her head a few times, but more like she was attempting to clear her mind as opposed to answering no. She took her cell out of her pocket, pushed a couple of keys, and put the phone to her ear. After a long moment, she shook her head and disconnected. "No answer."

"You okay?"

"I've got that position, looks like they were on Highway 29, in central Wisconsin. Five, maybe six miles outside of the town of Wausau."

"Can you enlarge that map slightly?"

Iggy clicked a couple of keys, and the map on his screen enlarged to a point where the names of some towns were legible. Highway 29 itself was clearly displayed, and there was a blue star indicating the point where the call had been placed.

"Bonnie, look at this. Is it anywhere near where your sister's place is?"

She looked at the map for a moment, then said, "No, she's actually further east and north. But that's the route we take. I'd guess her place is maybe a good hour, hour-and-a-half away."

"Think they're heading back here?"

"They certainly could be. I just don't know."

"Try your sister again. Iggy, is there any way to track them?"

"No, well, unless they've brought a unit along that I'm embedded in. That's highly unlikely. I'm checking now, but nothing so far," he said, then went back to clicking keys.

"Still no answer at my sister's," Bonnie said.

"Okay, call the police for that area. Don't mention anything about the kids. Just tell them you've been trying to reach her, she hasn't answered and could they drive out and check."

"They'll get there faster if we tell them about Wegger's call."

Iggy shook his head but continued tapping keys. "And then we have no way of knowing what he's likely to do if the police confront him. At least this way, we've still got a chance, he'll work with us."

Bonnie seemed to think about that for a moment, then picked up her iPad and moved her fingers around. "Lily's the name of the town. It's a little place, God, it's an unincorporated town. It says here there isn't one, a police department."

"Check the county."

"It's Langlade County, umm, I think Crandon City might be the closest one. I'm calling them now."

I turned back to Iggy, "Anything?"

"I've got two more units to check, long shots. I'm probably going to come up empty-handed."

"If you can't find—"

Bonnie was talking to someone. "Yes, I'm hoping you could help me," she sniffled but seemed to be keeping it all together, at least for the moment. "I've been trying to reach my sister, she has a place on the Lily

River, I'm not getting an answer, and I'm hoping you might be able to send someone out to check on her. What? Yes, she does have a medical condition, she has a heart condition, and she's diabetic. Yes, oh, thank you so very much. Here's her phone number," Bonnie gave them the phone number, her sister's address and then, finally, her cellphone number. "Yes, I'm calling from Minnesota, the Twin Cities. Thank you, no, no, I really appreciate your help," she said, then hung up. "They'll send someone out to check, but it's probably going to be a few hours."

"Chrissy has a heart condition?"

"What? Oh, no, I just made that up, so I didn't sound like some neurotic woman who didn't get a response to her Facebook post. No, my sister's as healthy as a horse, or at least she was," and the tears suddenly welled up in her eyes again.

Iggy turned around, faced her, and in a voice I hadn't heard before said, "Bonnie, we're going to deal with this. Everything is going to be okay. Now, I'm going to need you at this keyboard over here. Yeah, right, now enter this code," he said as Bonnie sat down in front of the computer. He read off a bunch of numbers and letters signifying upper and lower case on the letters. "That's at least one of the systems in Wegger's office, and I think his lab. Put that headset on. I want you to go back forty-eight hours and begin listening to conversations. You might be able to pick up some idea of where they're heading to or, God forbid, some semblance of whatever foolish plan they've hatched."

Bonnie took a deep breath and began reviewing the taped conversations from Wegger's computer. Iggy was madly clicking keys. I went upstairs and found Luscious asleep in a lawn chair out on the deck. He had headphones on and an iPod resting on his chest. I kicked his foot a couple of times until he came awake.

"Luscious, bit of an emergency. I want you to check on something for me."

He yawned and said, "You can count on me, Dev."

"Perfect. Here's what I want you to do. Drive over to Wegger's house. I've got his address on the kitchen counter next to a bag of pretzels. See if his green Jaguar is in the driveway. Now that I think of it, even if it's not in the driveway, knock on the door, see if Wegger answers. Let me know either way if he's home or not."

"You want me to bring him back here, Dev?"

"That's tempting, but it would probably be better if you didn't. Take Bonnie's car. The keys are hanging on the cabinet by the kitchen sink."

"I'm on the job, Dev."

"Thanks, Luscious, I'm counting on you, and for God's sake, drive carefully." A moment later, I heard him grab the car keys, then heard him rip the pretzel bag open as he headed down the stairs and out the door.

Thirty-six

Bonnie's phone rang about forty-five minutes later. It was sitting on the desktop alongside the computer she was working on. With the head-phones on, she didn't appear to hear it ringing. I stepped over and tapped her on the shoulder, then said, "Phone," and pointed to her cellphone on the desktop.

"Yeah, I know. It's Wayne. I'm ignoring it."

"Wayne? Maybe he's got information."

"Believe me, Wayne doesn't have any information, certainly nothing worth listening to."

"I don't know, Wegger, the kids, maybe he knows something."

The cellphone stopped ringing at this point, and Bonnie said, "Didn't you tell me Wegger assaulted him in Benny's? You said he threatened Wayne, told him he wanted his hundred dollars back, right?"

"It still might be worth checking out just to be sure," I said.

"I suppose it couldn't hurt. Thus far, the only thing of interest on these tapes has been an order for pizza and one side of an obscene phone call with some woman named Celeste." She picked up her cellphone, pressed a couple of keys, and waited.

"Hello, Wayne. Sorry I missed your call. I was busy working. What can I do for you? Really? And why now? I see. Well, other than your illegal entry a few days ago and your apologetic phone call, I haven't heard from you for the past three-plus years, so I don't think we're interested. No, Wayne, I, I won't reconsider. Wayne, Wayne," she said and then burst into tears, crying uncontrollably.

I took the cellphone from her hand. "Hello."

"Who the hell is this?"

"Dev Haskell, Wayne. We met last week out on the deck. Remember, you gave me the finger when you drove off, that was right after I helped you into your truck. I saw you the following night at Benny's. Niles Wegger pushed you into a couple of bar stools before I had a chance to get my hands on you."

"Oh, yeah. You're the guy who snuck up, then blindsided me with that board."

"You mean the guy who opened the door for you when you were trying to break in, then broke your nose, just on general principles."

"What's going on over there? Is Bonnie okay?"

"She's just under a lot of pressure right now and really busy."

"Then put one of the kids on."

"They're all outside playing. Look, if there's nothing else—"

"Listen, wise-ass, I've been pretty patient up till now. I got half a mind—"

"Stop right there, Wayne. You're absolutely right. You do have half a mind. Unfortunately, it seems to be the pain in the ass half. Please don't call for a couple of days. Bonnie's working on a project and doesn't need the interruption."

"You can't tell me—" I disconnected and handed the cellphone back to Bonnie.

"I don't know, Dev," Bonnie sniffled. "He's tried to be really nice ever since you cracked him over the head with that board."

"Well, there you go. Maybe a half-dozen more therapy sessions like that, and he'll be halfway normal."

"Maybe," she said, then slipped the headphones back on.

They continued working, probing, listening, tapping keys, and coming up empty-handed over the course of the next three hours. "Let's break for a moment and put our heads together," Iggy said, rolling his chair away from a keyboard and into the middle of the room.

Bonnie let off a long sigh, pulled off her headphones, and rolled away from the computer. I shook my head in an effort to come fully awake.

"The problem, as I see it, is we give them access tonight, and they can embed something we'll probably never be able to find. That said," Iggy stared at Bonnie. "We're going to give them access, your children and your sister are first priority. We all want them back, safe, and sound."

"Can't you just duplicate this, store it in a closet or something? Let Wegger embed whatever it is and then delete the thing, and you know, use the duplicate program," I said.

"I think you meant store it in the cloud."

"If you say so, but wouldn't that work?"

"It's a good idea except for one little problem. It won't work. Wegger will embed his bug in a number of places. Even if we delete it, he'll have it programmed to re-embed. Visualize a hornet just hovering out there somewhere and programmed to sting you the moment you step outside. Now, you can change clothes, wear a disguise, but he's still going to hover, and no matter how much you disguise yourself, alter your appearance, height, voice, maybe hair color, gait, even your acquaintances, your DNA always remains constant. Which means you're still going to get stung. Once Wegger obtains access to our systems, he essentially has our program's DNA. And, therefore, continual access."

My cellphone rang, it was Luscious. I took the call. "Luscious, what did you find out?"

"The car is in the driveway, it's that fancy dark green Jaguar, right?"

"Yeah, did you check to see if he was home?"

"I knocked, rang the doorbell, then went around to the back door and knocked. No one answered. When I peeked through the window of the front door, there was some mail on the floor, so I'm pretty sure no one's home. You want me to sneak inside?"

Luscious 'sneaking' inside would probably amount to something subtle like a brick thrown through a large picture window. "No, better not, more risk involved for very little benefit. Come on back here, and we'll figure out what we're going to do next."

I hung up and looked at Bonnie and Iggy. "I sent Luscious over to check out Wegger's place."

"I think Wegger is liable to be a bit more cautious than carrying on like this in his home," Iggy said.

"I agree, but it doesn't hurt to be sure. Anyway, Luscious didn't find anything. No one seems to be home, mail scattered on the floor inside the front door, and Wegger's Jaguar was parked in the driveway."

"What does that mean?" Bonnie asked

"Well, it means he's not home, and he's not driving his Jaguar. So either he has another vehicle or, at the very least, access to one, and that ups the possibility that he has at least one accomplice."

"What about his brother, the one who escaped the other night?" Bonnie asked.

"His name is Delmar," Iggy added.

"I'd say the odds are rather high. Let me make a call to a contact I have at the DMV and check on vehicles registered to the two of them."

Iggy glanced at his watch. "It's after four, in less than five hours, we're going to have to let them gain access to our systems." He sounded more than a little frustrated.

"I just want my babies safe," Bonnie said, then picked up her phone and clicked it on. It immediately chimed a half-dozen times. "Oh, God, it looks like Wayne has been calling nonstop."

"Can you get rid of him?" I asked. "We really don't need any more complications at this stage."

"I'll try, I'm sure he just wants to help. After all, they're his kids too."

"Bonnie. He doesn't even know. He hasn't…"

"I know, I know, it's just that it's the only interest he's ever shown since, well, forever. It's actually kinda nice, in a Wayne way, if that's possible."

Thirty-seven

onnie was in the process of returning Wayne's call when the doorbell rang. We all looked at one another.

"Wegger," Iggy said.

"The kids," Bonnie said and jumped from her seat.

Morton barked.

"Oh, God, now what," I groaned.

I was two steps behind Bonnie as she raced up the stairs to the front door. "Bonnie, Bonnie, will you hold on for a minute, wait. We don't know who it is." Too late, she pulled the door open just as I reached the top of the stairs.

"Oh. Wayne, it's just you," she said, not hiding her disappointment.

"Hey, Baby, you okay? I brought you some pizza, look, your favorite. Sausage with anchovies and plain cheese with extra cheese just for the kids."

"Kind of a bad time right now, Wayne."

Wayne looked over her shoulder and sneered at me. The rectangular bruise on his forehead was still there, but not so purple, more of a light blue with tinges of green and brown around the edges. He still had a splint on his nose, but it was half the size of the one he wore the last time I saw him. The swelling had gone down around his eyes, and they were no longer purple. In fact, the black rings just made him look kind of tired and over-worked, not that he ever did anything.

"What the hell is he still doing here? You're the bas-tard that assaulted me, ain't you? I wasn't holding these pizzas I brought for the lady, you and me would have ourselves a little discussion, and by the time…"

"Wayne, shut the hell up. We got problems, and Dev here is helping us. So please. Shut. Up."

"Sure, baby, anything you say."

"And I'm not your baby."

"Oh, yeah, sorry, I forgot. Hey, maybe I can help. What's the problem?"

"Bonnie, don't," I said.

"Dev, he's bound to find out sooner or later. We seem to be stuck wondering what the hell we're going to do. Is one more person trying to figure out what's hap-pening going to set us back?"

"We're not even sure whose side he's on," I said.

"Maybe I could tell you if you'd give me half a chance. What? I suppose he went and knocked you up. It's just lucky for you, I'm—"

"Wayne, shut up," Bonnie shouted. "If you're going to help, I want you to shut up. You are the last person in control here. You got it? Well, do you?"

"Yes, ma'am."

"I mean it, Wayne, the very last. Okay. Much better, now bring those pizzas downstairs, and no, I'm not pregnant. By the way, that's Iggy down there on the computers. Say hello and nothing else, and I'm not kidding."

As Wayne hurried past, he gave me a look that suggested something along the lines of, 'You just wait.' I heard him say, "Hello, I brought you some pizza," as he entered Iggy's room.

A half-second later, Iggy called, "Bonnie? Dev?"

* * *

I was on my second piece of pizza. Wayne had been repeating, "I can't believe they've been kidnapped," for the past ten minutes. I'd been on hold for almost the same amount of time, waiting for Donna at the DMV to pick up. Suddenly, she was on the other end of the line and sounding very flustered.

"This is Donna, is she all right?"

"Oh, hi, Donna, actually it's Dev Haskell. I wanted to get…"

"Are you kidding me? They told me it was my daughter's school calling. They said she'd been in an accident. What in the hell are you doing at her school?"

"I'm sorry. The receptionist must have misunderstood me?"

"Oh, God. You got me out of an important meeting for this nonsense. I'm going to hang up right—"

Mike Faricy ♦ 194

"Donna, Donna, calm down. This is serious. There's been an incident. It does not involve your daughter, but we suspect there have been some children kidnapped. I need some information."

"Kidnapped? Oh, my God. Why is it that you— wait just a minute, here. If you're working with the police, why call me? They can access our files probably faster than I can."

"I'm not working with the police. The family is afraid to go to them just now. Can you just look up two names? We're just trying to find out if they have access to additional vehicles."

"So help me God, if I find out you're lying to me, I don't care if you do report me for the one dalliance you know about. I'll report you, and make sure you go to jail. I just happen to have contacts, too."

"Fair enough. Here are the two names, Niles Wegger and—"

"Isn't that the same name you asked me about the other day?"

"Yes, you checked out his license number and gave me his name and address. I need to know if he or a brother named Delmar Wegger have access to any other vehicles besides that Jaguar."

"So help me," she said, but I could hear her working the keys on her keyboard. "Okay, there is a second vehicle registered to Niles Wegger. A 2015 Cadillac Escalade, Crystal Red Tint Coat in color, so it's red. I'm not finding any reference to a Delmar by that last name."

There was a pause as I heard more keys clicking. "No, I've tried a number of different spellings, M-A-R, M-E-R, D-E-L, double L, nothing coming up."

"Can you give me a license number on that Escalade?"

"It's a Minnesota personalized plate, E-G-G-H-E-A-D."

"Egg Head?"

"That's correct, with no space, just one word."

"Donna, thank you for your help. I really mean it. Maybe watch for this on the news."

"As I said before, God help you, if you're trying to pull one of your usual stunts, I'll see you behind bars."

"Thanks, Donna," I said and hung up. "Okay, we've got a vehicle and a license. Now we just need to watch his house and hope he goes there."

"In the meantime, I'd better get prepared. If we can't stop him, we're going to give him access and just pray for the best," Iggy said.

"You all talking about that bastard, Niles Wegger?" Wayne asked. He was in the process of tilting his head back and holding a piece of cheese pizza above his mouth. Not unlike the way you might feed a seal.

"What if we are?" Bonnie asked.

"Well, it just seems to me that if he's trying to pull something fancy, he ain't gonna use his house as a hideout, I mean, you know." Then he lurched his head up and snapped off maybe a third of the piece of pizza before he looked around and smiled at the three of us.

"Wayne, honey," Bonnie said. "Are you trying to tell us something we don't know?"

"I don't think so, y'all know 'bout his other place on the St. Croix, don't you?" he said, then took another huge bite of pizza.

We looked at one another, then together turned and focused on Wayne. His head was tilted back, and he was about to go for a third bite of pizza.

"Wayne, honey, tell your babydoll more."

"That place he's got down on the St. Croix River, it's a big fancy joint. I was down there with some guys, partying. Niles had us down for the night. It was really great," he said, then lurched upwards and snatched the remainder of the pizza from his hand.

Thirty-eight

The St. Croix River marks the border between Minnesota and Wisconsin for a hundred and twenty-five miles. It's designated as a natural scenic river-way and falls under the protection of the National Park Service. It would be the perfect place from which to launch Wegger's plan of bugging Iggy's programs and conducting a release of Bonnie's kids.

"He's got a place on the St. Croix?"

"Hello. Yeah. He brought a bunch of us out there one night. Had these girls come in. Let me tell you, they— Oh, sorry, Bonnie. I mean, that's just what I heard, you know, from some of the guys."

"Shut up, Wayne. Believe me, I So. Do. Not. Care."

"Wayne, you've been out to his place on the St. Croix?" I asked.

Wayne gave a nervous glance toward Bonnie for a moment, grinned, shook his head from side to side, and said, "Well, yeah." Suggesting something like 'Who wouldn't want Wayne at their place?'

"Is this close to town or way up north?"

"Pretty close to town, I'd say. I mean, Niles rented a limo and hauled all of us out there. Trip back is kinda fuzzy and all. Pretty good time from what I can remember. See, there was this one redhead…”

“Wayne, you think you could find it again? Take us there?”

“I suppose, ‘course the girls don’t live there or anything. Not sure there’d be a party going on tonight. They was just brought in as entertainment, see.”

“Yeah, I get it. Look, I’m serving no purpose here,” I said. “If Wayne and I went out there to this place on the St. Croix, we might have a chance. It makes sense, Wegger almost has to pass by the place to get home. Better he stays out there. I’m guessing it’s secluded, private. Iggy, would it make sense he could gain access to your systems from out there?”

“From what I know of Wegger,” Iggy said, rattling his sheet of Mylar, “he wouldn’t be anywhere that didn’t have access. It makes perfect sense to me. In fact, let me search county records and see if I can obtain an address. It should only take a minute,” he said and spun around in his chair.

“Oh, Wayne, if you can get the kids back…” Bonnie said, then fell into another bout of crying.

“I’ll get em, back,” he said, then stepped over and wrapped his arms around her. He shot me a look that suggested something like, ‘Look what I got and I’m not sharing,’ then he proceeded to subtly wipe his hands off on the back of her olive-drab t-shirt, leaving a trail of pizza grease.

"If they're not there by now, they're liable to be there pretty soon," Iggy said.

"But what if they're not planning to go there? What if he goes to his house? Or he gets a hotel room or something?" Bonnie cried.

"For this particular transaction, he almost has to go somewhere that's under his control. A commercial establishment like a hotel, a library, or an educational institution is too risky, and the actions would be traceable. An internet cafe would be even worse. No," Iggy said. "It almost has to be his home or this other place out on the St. Croix."

"Come on, Wayne, we're wasting time just cooling our heels here," I said and headed for the door.

"Now, you just hold on a minute. I'm the one who came up with this idea. I'm the one who knows where in the hell this place is at. I think I'm the one should play the boss here. You see what I'm saying?" he said, looking at Bonnie.

"Basically, you're saying you're an idiot," Bonnie said.

"Listen, Baby, I think…"

"Stop right there, Wayne. Please don't think. I want Dev to go with you. This isn't some stupid game we've been playing for the last four hours. This is serious. Now, take Dev with you and do whatever he tells you to do. He's the boss."

"But, Baby, I think—"

"Wayne!" she screamed.

We all jumped, Iggy pulled the Mylar tighter around his shoulders.

"Okay, okay, he can come with."

"When Luscious comes back, bring him up to speed, then tell him to watch the backyard. If, for some unknown reason, Wegger does happen to show up here, he'll either have to ring the doorbell or try and sneak in the back. You'll have him, either way. I've got my cell, contact me with any changes."

"You be careful, Dev," Bonnie said. Then, as an afterthought, added, "You, too, Wayne."

"Don't worry," I said. "The key is the kids. That's our goal. We'll make sure they're safe. That's the mission, the important thing, the only important thing. Okay?"

Bonnie and Iggy nodded. Wayne gave me a disgusted look, then mumbled, "Whatever, man. Come on, let's get going."

Thirty-nine

I followed Wayne out the door and up the stairs. He opened the front door and hurried to his truck, which was parked across the driveway, effectively blocking anyone with the idea of coming or going. He was behind the wheel and turning the ignition as I walked around the front of the vehicle. Just as I reached for the handle on the passenger door, the truck lurched forward, and the door swung open. I jumped inside and pulled myself into the seat as the door slammed closed.

"Thought I had you there for a minute," he said, then turned up the volume on the radio, some country rock song was playing, with a guy moaning off-key because he'd been dumped by his girlfriend. There were three empty beer cans rolling around the floor on the passenger side. I stomped my foot on them, one after the other then picked them up off the floor.

"You're pretty tough when it comes to empty beer cans," Wayne said.

I tossed the flattened cans into the backseat. "You know, Wayne. I'm sorry I hit you with that board the way I did. And I'm sorry I broke your nose. I should have hit you a hell of a lot harder with the board and knocked some sense into that thick skull of yours. Then, after I broke your nose, I should've busted your jaw."

He looked at me, wide-eyed. The guy on the radio sang, "Go ahead and kiss him, see if I care."

"Now this isn't some game we're playing. There's a good chance someone's going to get hurt," I said, then pulled my pistol out from behind my back, checked the chamber, and stuck the weapon back in my belt. "Let's make sure it's not you or me and certainly not one of the kids. Okay?"

He didn't say no. As a matter of fact, he didn't say anything until he pulled onto the interstate and headed east. "You didn't have to break my nose, man."

"Okay, first of all, I didn't know who you were. Second, you were in the process of breaking into Bonnie's house. Third, you asked me if I thought I was tough. Fourth, you threatened to sue me. You know, at some point, you keep pushing, you're just going to run out of luck and end up with your nose in a splint."

"You got any idea what a pain in the ass this has been for me?"

"Pain in the…Wayne. You're lucky we didn't call the cops on you. Didn't Bonnie file a restraining order on you? I mean, technically you're in violation just for bringing those pizzas over this afternoon."

"Hey, man. It hasn't exactly been easy for me, you know."

"Yeah, you're telling me, she built a business from the ground up. She and Iggy have developed this program that the folks out in Seattle seem to be really interested in. She's been raising three little kids all by herself. She—"

"Dude, in case you weren't listening, I was talking about me."

"Maybe that's a big part of the problem, Wayne. You've been so busy trying to be cool, you've done absolutely nothing to help your family."

Neither one of us spoke after that. I noticed he had two naked girl air fresheners hanging from the dash and another one sitting on the console. I was about to say something, then remembered the little farewell gift I'd left on the floor the night I broke his nose.

He didn't say anything until we were almost at the St. Croix River and just about to head over the river bridge and into Wisconsin. He took the last exit, just before the bridge. He turned off the interstate onto St. Croix Trail and headed south toward the town of Afton. He gave me a sideways glance, then stared for a long moment.

"So, what do you haul your ass around in? I suppose something that's good for the environment."

"Me? God, no way. I drive an American machine, none of that foreign stuff for me."

"Oh?" He couldn't seem to hide the surprise in his voice. I'm sure the one-track mind was thinking an F-

150 just like him, maybe one of the Super-Duty truck models, a Humvee, or some gigantic SUV.

"Yeah, I've got a classic, an '87 Lancer."

"An '87... does it even run?"

"Most of the time. It was originally red, but, with the fading going on over the past almost thirty years now, it's kind of a bunch of different shades of pink."

"Pink?" he half-shouted and almost went off the road.

"Yeah, really stands out."

We drove through both blocks of the main street of Afton. Wayne cast a couple of sideways glances at me as we traveled past a couple of antique stores, an ice cream store, and some gift shops. He shook his head and mumbled, "Pink." A moment later, he said, "Okay, on one of these next roads, we take a left and head toward the river. I'm not exactly sure which one it is, but I'm pretty sure I'll know it when I see it," then he slowed down, maybe trying to remember.

"I got the address right here, says it's on River Hollow."

"That ain't any of these signs," he said, driving past the fourth or fifth turn. "I don't know, shit, maybe it's up ahead a ways?"

I glanced at the digital clock on the dash. It was getting close to eight. In case I had any doubt, dusk was fast approaching.

"I just remember we took a turn, maybe one of those back there, and then we took another one. We drove down a private road, for maybe a mile. I kind of remember gravel, I think, maybe."

"So what you're saying is, this River Hollow address is his private road, and you don't know how to get to his private road, right?"

"God, I thought I did. Honest."

"Let's head back to one of those shops or maybe the ice cream store and ask directions. We can't be the first people to get lost out here."

"I think I can find it," he said as we passed two more lanes, and he muttered, "That ain't it, least it didn't look like it."

"Come on, Wayne. Go back to town, and we can ask someone before it gets dark. Otherwise, we'll never find the place. Besides, things are supposed to go down at nine, that gives us barely more than an hour."

"I don't know, I think—"

"Wayne, turn this damn thing around, we're wasting precious time here."

He seemed to think about that for a quarter-mile, then pulled onto the shoulder and let some BMW shoot past before he pulled a U-turn and headed back into town. Thank God. He pulled to a stop in front of a gift shop. Although it was on Main Street, the two-story structure looked like a farmhouse from a hundred and fifty years ago and was painted a mauve color with white trim. There was a porch light on over the door and a long bench sitting in front of a giant picture window. A flower box ran the length of the picture window and was over-flowing with red geraniums and impatiens. Potted flow-ers sat on each of the three steps leading up to the front door. All sorts of little figures were arranged throughout the yard, and as soon as Wayne turned his truck off, I could hear wind chimes.

Forty

I opened the door and said, "Come on, let's go, man."

"You kidding? I wouldn't be caught dead in that place. Look at it."

"Wayne, we're lost. You don't know how to get where we want to go. It's getting dark. We're trying to rescue the kids, your kids. Now come on."

"No way, man."

"Okay, give me the keys."

"What?"

"You heard me. I said give me the keys."

"Are you kidding? I—"

I had my pistol out and pointed at his knee. "I will not hesitate, Wayne, honest to God. Now give me your damn keys. You can stay in your stupid truck, but give me the damn keys, now. Hurry the hell up, while I'm still in a good mood."

Wayne pulled the keys out of the ignition, tossed them at me and mumbled, "Asshole." Then he looked out the driver's window, pouting. I hurried into the gift shop.

The place was crammed with stuff, gifts for kids, for him, for her, gifts for grandma. I guessed Wayne probably wasn't the first guy to sit in his truck in front of the place. "I'm sorry, we're about to close," a pleasant voice said from behind the counter. She was a redhead, maybe mid-twenties and quite attractive, from what I could see of her.

"Actually, I was hoping you can help, we're in a hurry and lost, looking for an address. We could probably walk there from here if we knew the way."

She smiled. "I'm really bad at that kind of thing, but Penny might be able to help. Penny," she called. "Penny!"

A beaded curtain behind the counter parted, and a child of the sixties stepped out. Her gray hair was pulled back, then braided to somewhere down below her shoulders. She wore what looked like a long, ill-fitting dress that probably went all the way to the floor, although I couldn't tell because she was standing behind the counter. She had a ring through her nose, twenty or thirty bracelets around either wrist and piercings along the top of both ears that looked like a zipper. As she took three or four steps toward me, the bracelets rattled, and the scent of incense seemed to float into the room.

"This gentleman seems to be lost and is looking for an address."

"Yeah." I handed the paper with Wegger's address to the gorgeous redhead. She passed it on to the sixties hippie.

"Oh, yes, not the first time we've been asked about this place. I suppose another *party*?" she said and shot a disgusted look in my direction.

"No, just going to pick up three small children."

"Children? They let this individual near children?" she said, then looked over my shoulder and out the large picture window at Wayne sitting behind the wheel of his red Ford F-150 with the bright yellow flames painted across the hood. "You're not attending some crazy orgy-fest?"

"I don't know anything about that, ma'am. I'm just trying to get three little kids out of there as fast as I can."

She studied me for a long moment. "Well, I'm not too sure of the Karma I'm sensing. I can only hope you're on the level. Turn your truck around. Go three-quarters of a mile down the road. You'll come to a series of five streets, take a left on the third one. Stay on it until you run out of pavement, and you're on gravel. I believe this location is the second left once you're on the gravel. If you drive to the point where you can see the river, you've gone too far. Enjoy your trip," she said, sounding like she meant anything but then handed the paper to the redhead and pushed back through the beaded curtain.

"I'll see you to the door and lock up," the redheaded girl said. She opened the door for me, then in a soft voice said, "Sorry about that, she was at some party there where everyone threw their keys on the table and you just, well, ended up with whoever…except no one picked up her keys."

"Gee, I can't imagine why."

"Child of the sixties, in case you didn't pick that up."

"Yeah, well, thank you for your help."

She quickly looked over her shoulder, then half-whispered, "Hey, if you guys are having a party, I've got a couple of friends, we 'dance.' Two hundred bucks an hour."

"What?"

"You think I make enough to buy her out earning minimum wage here? Besides, 'dancing' is all tax-free."

Wayne honked the horn on the truck, then waved at us.

"I better go, we're running late."

"Just remember, I'll be stopping for one in the bar down the street, it's never too late for fun. Here, take my card, just in case." She handed me a business card, what looked like a brass pole was on one end of the card, and then the words, 'More than you can handle' looking like they'd just spun off the pole. A phone number was in the lower right corner.

"Thanks," I called over my shoulder as I hurried to the truck.

Wayne honked the horn again, then called, "Hey, Veronica," and waved at the redhead as I climbed in.

"You know her?"

"Almost positive she was one of the strippers at Wegger's that night. Got this tattoo that says 'Party Time' right above…"

"Come on, let's get going, you can tell me about it on the way. Make a U-turn and head back the way we came."

The redhead was still standing in the doorway, and Wayne honked one more time before chirping his tires while making a U-turn on Main Street and speeding out of town. The hippie's directions were right on the money. We turned left on the third street, then drove until we ran out of pavement. Maybe a quarter of a mile beyond was a gravel drive heading into the woods. A rural mailbox set on a post was next to the drive. The mailbox didn't have a name, but the address on the side was the same as the one Iggy had written down for me. Wayne began to pull into the drive.

"Wait a minute, don't go in there."

"It's where the kids are, ain't it?"

"I hope so, but we don't want to be driving up to the front door. No telling what he'll do to the kids, well, or us, for that matter. Pull further down the road, out of sight, and we'll go in through the woods. You got a weapon?"

"Ummm, not really." Wayne gave me a dejected look, then brightened and said, "Hey, I got me a softball bat in the back of the truck."

"That'll do, just watch where you swing that thing. Now, let's get moving. It's after eight, and God only knows how far we'll have to go through those woods."

Wayne grabbed his softball bat out of the back of the truck, and we started in through the woods, making our way parallel to the gravel trail. There was a good deal of undergrowth, vines, and a fair amount of mosquitoes. After about twenty minutes, we saw lights shining through the trees and headed in that direction. A few minutes later, we saw a massive, contemporary structure with cedar shake siding. There was a large shed off to the left of the building. A bright red Cadillac Escalade sat in the drive in front of an open attached garage door. The personalized license plate read EGGHEAD.

Forty-one

Wayne looked around and said, "This here's Wegger's joint. I'm sure of it. There's a big picture window on the other side that looks out onto the river. I remember because that's where the girls were dancing. See, Wegger, he had this great big coffee table, and that redheaded gal from the gift shop, Veronica, she was up there shaking and—"

"Let's see if we can spot the kids, Wayne."

We scanned the front of the structure but didn't see any movement outside, nor inside, for that matter. We moved around the side. There were only three smaller windows, all up close to the eaves. They looked like they were along the ceiling of the second floor, or maybe even on a third floor. No light shined from the windows, so we moved around to the back.

A large stone patio with an outdoor fireplace, a porch swing, and a large picnic table looked out onto the river shore. The patio was illuminated by a half-dozen spotlights. What was probably a boathouse with a stone foundation, cedar shake walls and roof rose up from the river shore. A boat dock of white metal decking rested on green posts set in the water and extended out into the river. A white pontoon boat, I guessed maybe twenty-five feet long, was tied alongside the dock.

The picnic table was a single slab of wood that looked like it was the center cut from what had been a very large tree. It was maybe five feet wide and about ten or twelve feet long. At one end sat three kids. I recognized J.D. He was actually sitting at the end of the table with his brother and sister on either side. They all seemed to be involved with iPads. I couldn't see Bonnie's sister, Chrissy, anywhere. Delmar Wegger sat a few seats away. He was sipping from a can of beer and had a number of empties scattered on the table in front of him. His head seemed to weave from side to side, and even just sitting there, he appeared fairly intoxicated.

"Thank God, there they are, let's grab 'em. I'm getting eaten alive out here. One swing and that dude is toast," Wayne said, then slapped a couple of mosquitoes and started to move out of the woods toward the kids.

I grabbed him by his belt and pulled him back. "Bonnie's sister isn't there."

"Chrissy? Screw it. She never liked me, anyway."

Who could really blame her? "I've got an idea, let's go back in front."

"What? You gotta be kidding me."

"No, come on, I want to shut this bastard down. It's getting close to nine."

"But…"

"Wayne, come on, we're gonna make you the hero on this, okay?"

"Well, okay, but you better not be bullshitting me."

We made our way back through the woods toward the front of the place. Still no sign of movement from inside the house, and I conjured up a picture of Niles Wegger sitting in front of a bank of computer screens, all displaying some large clock ticking away. The moment the clock struck nine, he would automatically connect to Iggy's system.

"Wayne, I want to check out that shed," I said once we were back in front of the place.

"Are you nuts? What the hell for? This is crazy. I'm going back to grab those kids, and then we are so out of here."

"I just want to check if there's a saw we could cut the power to the house, grab the kids, and find Chrissy."

"Yeah, and we could bake a cake, too. You're fucking crazy, man. Now, I'm grabbing those kids, and we're getting the hell out of here before anything else happens. I don't really give a damn about Bonnie's computer bullshit. And if Wegger tries to stop me, I'm going to knock him out of the park, too," he said, then jabbed me in the arm with his softball bat.

"Ten minutes, just give me that."

"I'm thinking you should—"

"Come on, hell, it will take you a good five just to get back there."

"Okay, okay, but you better make it fast. I've wasted too much time on you already."

"Thanks," I said and hurried across the drive to the large shed. The door was locked with a brass padlock, but a key was in the base of the lock. I turned it, and the padlock opened. I pulled the door open, stepped inside, then pulled it partway closed, hoping it would still let some light in. Unfortunately, there just wasn't that much light to let in at this hour. I rutted around in the dark, stumbled into a lawnmower, a number of shovels, hand tools, a stack of paving bricks next to a snowblower, and what I think was a tent. Then on the back shelf, I felt what had to be a chainsaw. I grabbed it, along with a plastic gas can, hurried out of the shed and down the gravel drive. I'd seen three phone poles heading into the property from the road with the power line attached. After a few minutes, I spotted one not far off the drive.

I hurried alongside the pole, gave the chainsaw a half-dozen pulls before it coughed, and finally fired up. I cut a large notch in the pole, heard something snap, and then nothing. I stepped to the other side of the pole and cut straight across to the center of the notch. There was another snap, and the pole jumped up, sailed a few feet from the stump, dragged across the ground, and then did absolutely nothing. It just stood there still connected to the power line, wobbling back and forth. I kicked it a couple of times, and it moved ever so slightly, but that was all.

I followed the line further out toward the road until I came to the next phone pole and repeated the procedure. The same thing happened, only this time, once I cut it, the pole jumped twice as far then just leaned at a forty-five-degree angle wobbling up and down. I set the chainsaw at about the five-foot mark and began to cut through the pole again. The pole suddenly cracked, reversed direction, ripped the chainsaw out of my hand, then swung back again, knocking me to the ground. A moment later, there was a loud crack and a flash back near the house, and then everything was quiet.

I looked around for the chainsaw but couldn't find it. After a brief moment, I hurried to the drive and ran back toward the house. I was almost on top of it before I saw the thing. All the lights were off. I'd managed to cut the power. I heard something off to the right and ducked alongside the Cadillac. Wegger suddenly ran out the front door and around the side of the house

I followed him around the side of the house and onto the back patio. He was heading for the kids when I shouted and pulled my pistol. "Stop right there, or so help me, I'll shoot."

Wegger turned, raised his hands, then started walking backward. "I'm not sure you want to do that, Haskell. You miss and hit one of these children, it won't be very pretty," he said, then suddenly bounded off of the patio and into the darkness. I hurried toward the kids, Stella and Buddy were crying. J.D. looked like he was about to. Delmar appeared to be passed out in his chair.

"It's okay, guys, it's okay. We're safe. We're going to go home."

Wayne suddenly stumbled out of the woods. "I, I was just about to get him, then you got in the way."

"You see Chrissy anywhere?" I asked.

"Hey, I got these here kids, she's a big girl, she can just take care of herself."

"I think she's still in the boat," J.D. said. "That mean guy tied her to one of the chairs when we got here."

"Like I said, she can take care of herself. Lord knows, she never done me no favors," Wayne said, then looked around nervously.

"You just get these kids back to their mother."

"You ain't got to tell me twice. Come on, kids, let's go see your mom. Maybe take them things with, consider it a little present from me. Okay?" Wayne said.

J.D. gave him a funny look but picked up all three iPads. Wayne tucked Buddy under his arm and said, "I think I done enough around here." He glanced up at the far corner of the house, looking toward the second-floor window. "Man that Veronica gal on that coffee table. I tell ya—"

"Maybe get these kids home, Wayne. It's been kind of a crazy day. Wegger is out there somewhere. I'm going to try and find him."

That last statement seemed to get Wayne's attention, and he glanced around nervously. "I guess you're right, better get them back to their mom," he said, then hurried around the corner carrying Buddy while J.D. grabbed Stella's hand and followed.

Forty-two

I walked out to the edge of the patio and looked toward the river. It was dark, although I was able to make out the boathouse down along the shore. There were a handful of solar lights stuck in the ground around the patio. They gave off a little light but not much.

Delmar, sitting in a chair at the picnic table, hadn't moved an inch during all the commotion. A number of beer cans were scattered across the table, and two were on the ground under his chair. His feet rested on a cooler, and his head was tilted back, snoring. Suddenly, a heavy gurgling sound came from down by the river, and in the next moment, the engines on the pontoon boat throttled up, and it headed out into the river.

I ran down to the river and out onto the dock, but all I could do was watch the night lights on the pontoon fade toward the middle of the river. My cellphone rang a moment later.

"Yeah."

"Dev, are you okay?"

"Yeah. What about…"

"Wayne just called, he rescued the kids and got the power to Wegger's cut off. He's bringing them home and said you were lost in the woods and…"

"No, I'm not lost in the woods. I'm watching Wegger head down the river in a pontoon boat. He doesn't seem to be in any special hurry. Did he get access to your computers?"

"He was on for less than a minute when he suddenly went offline. Iggy's trying to find that particular system he was on but hasn't been successful. I never thought I'd ever say this, but thank God for Wayne."

"Yeah, something you don't hear every day. He's bringing the kids back to you, right?"

"Yes."

"Okay, call the police, get them involved, let them know what's happened. The sooner we get Wegger locked up, the better. I'm going to try and get Chrissy."

"Be careful," Bonnie said. I disconnected and hurried back to the house. Delmar was still snoring in the chair. I went in through a patio door and attempted to get my bearings. There were a half-dozen laptops arranged on two desks positioned against the wall. I unplugged the laptops, then stacked them up and carried them over to a couch. I slid them under the couch, then wandered around the room as my eyes began to adjust, looking for a way up to the second floor.

I found a staircase that led me up to a large living room. One entire wall was all glass and looked out onto the river. There were a number of lights out on the water, and it was impossible to tell which one of them was Wegger's pontoon boat. I noticed the coffee table in the corner Wayne had mentioned. To the right was a kitchen area, open to the living room.

I hurried over and ran my hands across the white marble counters, searching for car keys. I found a set hanging by a hook on the side of the refrigerator, grabbed them, and headed out the front door. I clicked the button on the keys, mercifully the lights blinked, and the Escalade chirped.

I hopped in behind the wheel, fired the car up, threw it in reverse, then spun around and hurried out the drive. I picked up speed once I reached the pavement, then hurried into town. I had no idea where the police station was, or even if there was one, but I could see the bar Veronica had mentioned. I could only hope she wasn't a fast drinker.

I pulled across the street and skidded to a stop, parking against traffic in a handicapped parking zone, not that there was any traffic. I hurried in the door and couldn't tell if the place was a hundred years old or some new joint just made to look like that. There was a couple in a booth who looked at me as I rushed in, the woman whispered something to the guy, and then they both just stared. Two guys at the bar sitting a couple of stools apart didn't bother to look up but just continued to stare at their beers. There were three young guys standing and laughing at the far end of the bar. I just caught sight of a redhead in the middle of them and hurried over in their direction.

"Veronica, hey, Veronica," I called.

Two of the guys looked at me, one of them took a couple steps forward to run interference. "Hey, easy pal, she's busy, private party."

Veronica's head popped out from behind. "Oh, this is the guy I was just telling you about. You get those kids?" she laughed.

"Yeah, but he's got a hostage. How do I get to the police station?"

The smile suddenly dropped from her face. "The police station? There isn't one."

"Washington County Sheriff's Department handles everything down here. They're headquartered up in Stillwater," the one who stepped in front of me said.

"They got a boat? The guy I'm after headed down-river in a pontoon boat and I—"

"Man, are you on the level?" one of the other guys asked.

"Yeah. This guy kidnapped three kids and their aunt. Look, I'm a private investigator. He's still got the woman, their aunt. Guy used to work for a government agency. He's a computer geek. I need to get out on that river and find them."

"God, by the time they get a boat out of Stillwater and down here, he could be already in Red Wing or up in St. Paul."

"Shit. You guys know someone with a boat?"

"You're really serious, man. Aren't you?"

"This guy is desperate. He's liable to kill this woman. He's going to get nailed for kidnapping. I'm not joking. Do you know how I can get my hands on a boat?"

"Well, I got one," the guy behind Veronica said. He hadn't spoken until this point.

"Can I borrow it? Look, I'll pay you. I got maybe a couple hundred bucks on me. I can get more. But I need to get moving."

He seemed to think about that for a moment, then looked at his two pals, who just shrugged. "No, I can't let you take it." Veronica shot him a glance. "But I'll drive you, and we can try and find them."

"You're not going alone, Tommy."

"Hey, guys, I'm serious, and I'm out of time. If you can take me, great, but I've got to get moving, like now."

The guy who stepped in front of me drained his beer and said, "Let's go, man, this'll be cool."

"I'm parked out front."

The other two slid off their stools, placed their glasses on the bar, and started to head toward the door.

"I just have to go to the bathroom," Veronica said, then slid off her stool.

Forty-three

We all just stood there and watched as she sauntered toward the ladies' room in the back of the bar, apparently in no particular hurry. The moment she pushed open the door to the ladies room, one of the guys said, "Come on, let's get going," and we hurried out to the car.

I hopped in behind the wheel of the Escalade. "Where to?" I asked as they all climbed in.

"Turn around and head out of town, it's fifteen miles down the county road," a voice said from the back. We were doing eighty and picking up speed as I headed out of town.

"One of you guys call 911, get us connected to a dispatcher. I want them to know what we're doing."

"Seriously?"

"Yeah, see if we can't get them involved, but I don't want to wait."

"I got it," someone in the back said, and I heard the key tones on his phone. A moment later, he said. "Yeah, umm, see, we're just heading out of Afton, and we're about to go out onto the river and stop a kidnapping, and we wanted to let you know. What? No. Honest. Well, yeah, but just maybe half a beer."

"God," the guy in the front passenger seat said.

"No, I don't know. Well, see, this guy came into the bar and…"

"Have him give me that phone."

"Tommy, give the guy the phone."

"Here, hang on a minute, he wants to talk to you," he said, then passed the phone up to me.

"Hello, who am I speaking to?"

"This is the Washington County Sheriff's Department," the guy said in a no-nonsense tone. I expected him to read me the riot act for wasting his time. "This is an emergency number. Just what…"

"My name is Devlin Haskell. I'm a licensed private investigator in the State of Minnesota. I'm licensed to carry a weapon." Suddenly, you could hear a pin drop in the car. "Earlier this evening, I rescued three children who had been abducted along with their aunt. I'm in pursuit of a man named Niles Wegger." I spelled the name for him. "He's still holding the woman, Chrissy Lowry. They're heading down the St. Croix in a pontoon boat. I'm going after them."

"Sir, I can dispatch a Sheriff's Deputy and—"

"There isn't that kind of time. Call this number." I rattled off Bonnie's number. "It's Bonnie Lowry's number. She's the mother of the kidnapped children. She's already contacted the St. Paul Police."

"Sir, I'm going to have to insist that—"

"I'm sorry, but we don't have that kind of time."

"You are in violation of—"

"Take the next left up here, just on the other side of this hill," a voice said from the back.

"Look, I gotta go, call Bonnie's number," I said and clicked the phone off. We shot up the small hill, then went airborne for a moment or two at the top before we landed back on pavement.

"Left turn is right here," the voice said, and I slammed on the brakes. We skidded past the road, and I threw the car in reverse. I pushed it into drive, and we headed down the road. With the tree branches arched overhead, it was like driving through a tunnel. I flicked on the brights and started to pick up speed.

"It gets really curvy up ahead, and then you get to our place, so better hold your speed down." He wasn't kidding. I sailed past a yellow road sign that signaled a series of 'S' curves and then hit the brakes as we wound our way through.

"Right after this next curve is our mailbox, take a left just on the far side."

I did as I was told, and we suddenly pulled in front of a 1960s rambler. As we hopped out, the guy who'd been giving me directions called, "This way," and headed across a grassy hill and down toward the river.

I could see a dock jutting out into the water. It was shaped like a 'T' and had three boats tied to it. There was a large pontoon boat similar to the one Wegger had taken, maybe a little smaller, an aluminum fishing boat with an outboard hanging on the back, and then a slick-looking speedboat. We ran down to the metal dock, then thundered across it to the speedboat. One of the guys began untying the boat while the rest of us climbed aboard. He hopped in over the side just as the boat started, and we headed out onto the river.

"You said this guy was driving a pontoon?"

"Yeah. It's Tommy, right?" I said to the guy behind the wheel.

"Yeah, nice to meet you. Never met a private investigator before."

I nodded. "Can't tell you how much I appreciate this. He was headed downriver from up in Afton. Didn't seem to be in a hurry, just took his time heading out to the middle of the river, then turned and headed downstream."

"Maybe he didn't want to call attention to himself, who knows? He can get some speed, but nothing like this. We can do up to fifty knots if we have to."

I gave him a blank look.

"That's about sixty miles per hour."

"A speedboat," I said.

"Not exactly. It's a jet boat, runs on water propulsion rather than a prop, and has a shallow draft. Let's check these guys out," he said, then pushed the throttle down and sped toward the set of lights far up ahead of us just as clouds were beginning to form.

Forty-four

It wasn't Wegger. Nor was the next boat, or the two after that.

"Shit, man, it's after ten, and everyone is heading home or pulling into a camping site. Not a lot of movement."

He wasn't kidding. There was a set of lights far behind us, most likely one of the three boats we'd already checked. Off on the Wisconsin side of the shore a couple of boats had pulled up onto the sand, and someone had built a large fire, you could see five or six people standing around, probably planning to spend the night.

"You think maybe we were ahead of them when we started out, and he's back behind us somewhere?" I asked.

Tommy just shrugged. "Tough to say. We've been making pretty good time, so he couldn't be much further ahead if he kept that leisurely pace. Course, he could have pulled into shore somewhere, and we would have shot right past him. Kind of a guessing game, but you can see how light the traffic's getting. And it looks like the weather's about to turn to shit."

I didn't want to admit it, but he was right. Just two sets of lights up ahead, the furthest one was so far out it could have been a taillight on a parked car, not that I could tell. Then, just in case things weren't screwed up enough, it started to rain.

"How 'bout we check those two out up ahead?" I said. "We don't find anything, I don't know, maybe head back, check along the shore as we go. I'm open to any ideas at this point."

"We'll check those two up ahead. Tell you the truth. I can't believe he'd be this far down. We're almost to Prescott, where it flows into the Mississippi. He gets that far, he can head in a number of different directions. With this weather, I'd say just a couple more minutes, then we better turn around. Sorry, man."

With that, he pushed the throttle forward and picked up speed, heading downriver. We came up close to the first set of lights. Tommy backed off the speed as we came abreast of an expensive-looking cabin cruiser. The guy driving looked over at us, raised a beer can, and gave a toast. Tommy waved back, pushed the throttle forward, and we took off downriver toward the last set of lights.

One of the guys sitting in back stepped forward and said, "Any luck? We're thinking we should maybe consider heading back upriver before this rain really kicks in. Sorry, but it looks like you might have drawn a blank."

I just frowned and nodded.

"Yeah, we're gonna check this last bastard up ahead. If he ain't our boy, we're heading back," Tommy said.

We pulled closer over the next few minutes. But once we were in sight, I looked at it and said, "Damn it, I don't think that's him."

"No shit? God, I was hoping. Damn, it's the first pontoon we've seen."

I took another look. "That's a pontoon? It doesn't look like the one he was driving. His was mostly white, and didn't have that black top."

"That's a Bimini top, it's just canvas on a metal frame, usually for protection against the sun. It probably works, at least a little in this mist, but this rain gets any heavier it's worthless. If he picks up any speed, it can become a real hazard. Come on, we'll just check it out," Tommy said and sped up until he was parallel with the pontoon boat. "You see anything that looks familiar?"

"No, I can't see shit, maybe—"

Suddenly the pontoon pushed forward. We were close enough to see the canvas top beginning to shake.

"Stupid bastard, what the hell does he think he's doing? He keeps that up he's going to bend his frame. If he doesn't rip that top off altogether."

"Can you get any closer?"

Tommy edged the throttle forward ever so slightly, and the jet boat seemed to jump. He turned the wheel toward the pontoon, and we moved closer for maybe five seconds before the first shot was fired.

"Jesus Christ," Tommy shouted, then swung the wheel around, and we did a 180 that sent me stumbling backward as we rocketed back upriver. "I'd say you found your man. Son of a bitch, now what?"

"Can you follow him, maybe hang back a bit, but stay on him." I pulled my phone out, looked at the screen, 'No Service.' The other two guys were suddenly down on the floor. One of them was hurriedly strapping on a lifejacket. "Hey, one of you guys got a phone?"

"Yeah, I got mine," the other one said.

"Call 911. Any way to tell where the hell we are out here?"

"Tell him we're about two miles upriver from Prescott, we're just passing the Meyer's place on the Minnesota side," Tommy yelled back.

A moment later, I heard the guy on the phone. "No, damn it, I already told you, a kidnapping. They're shooting at us. No. The guy's some kind of a detective. Okay, just a minute. Hey, here, take this, I guess he wants to talk to you," the guy said, crawling over to me on all fours. Tommy was hanging back, still following the pontoon.

"Yeah, hello."

"Are you the individual I spoke with earlier?"

"Yes. We're following the pontoon boat with a woman being held against her will. The guy driving the pontoon, his name is Niles Wegger, and he's armed. He's already fired at us."

"I want you to stop your pursuit immediately before someone gets hurt."

"He'll kill her for sure if we stop. Can you alert the police in Prescott to come upriver, maybe they could…"

There was a pause on the other end of the line, then he said, "Hold on. Bear with me while I put you through to Prescott. Let me talk first."

A moment later, a woman answered, "Prescott emergency services."

The Stillwater dispatcher went on to explain the situation. Told her what we were doing and asked if they could get someone moving upriver. "Hold a minute, let me contact," and she was suddenly off the line.

"Did she hang up on us?" I asked.

"No, I think she's probably going to contact their chief. He's actually got a boat and lives on the river. It would probably be the best option if he's home. We'll just have to—"

"Still there?" She was suddenly back.

"Yes," we answered at the same time.

"We're putting a boat in the water. He can be heading upriver in just a few minutes. Is there a way he can identify you?"

I thought for half a moment, then asked Tommy, "You got a spotlight or anything on here?"

"I've got a light on the bow and a couple of high-powered torches stored beneath one of the seats."

I repeated that to the dispatcher. "We'll turn them on and flash them, so he can see us as he approaches.

The pontoon we're following is maybe a hundred yards ahead of us, still heading downriver, closer to the Minnesota side."

Tommy yelled at the guys on the floor to check under the seats for the torches. Then he turned on his spotlight, and the beam shot into the darkness, maybe twenty feet off from the side of the pontoon. After a few seconds, he shut it off.

"Are these them?" the guy with the lifejacket called and held up what looked like two long flashlights.

"Yeah, that's them. Go back there and grab them," Tommy said to me. "Then head up to the bow, and you can shine them from there."

I stepped back and grabbed the torches, then headed for the bow. The two guys stayed back, curled up on the floor. Tommy continued to hold the same distance behind Wegger.

I knelt down in the bow, then clicked one of the torches on, it was like a laser beam shooting into the darkness of the river. I directed the beam onto the rear of the pontoon for a moment, caught what I think was Wegger, then flicked it off.

"He's picking up speed," Tommy called a moment later, and I felt the jet boat inch forward. I flicked the torch on again a half-minute later, the canvas top on the pontoon had risen on one side and looked to be flapping. I turned the torch off.

Forty-five

We kept it up for the next ten or fifteen minutes. At one point, I thought Wegger might be heading for shore, but in the end, he continued downriver. A white light, way beyond Wegger blinked in our direction, and Tommy yelled, "See that light flashing, I bet that's our guy, the Prescott cop." He flashed the spotlight, and I clicked the torch a couple of times in that direction, then flashed the torch on the pontoon.

The canvas top seemed to hang at an odd angle like maybe Wegger had tried to lower the thing, and it bent, or maybe the frame just happened to bend, given the speed he was moving at. As the torch illuminated the area, Wegger gave a quick glance back, then turned toward us and pointed a gun. I flicked off the torch, and a moment later, two shots echoed off the sides of the river valley. Tommy eased back on the throttle and flashed the spotlight downriver again.

The light coming toward us from downriver was growing closer, the Prescott cop must have had the thing moving all out. Tommy flashed the spotlight three times, and the light flashed back three times. The action didn't seem to be lost on Wegger, because the pontoon suddenly made a hard right and headed for shore.

"He's going to beach her," Tommy shouted.

I put the torch on the pontoon, Wegger was definitely heading into shore. I went back and forth, shining the torch on the pontoon, then out into the middle of the river at the boat charging toward us, hoping he could see the pontoon. After a couple of flashes, the approaching light veered toward the shore, heading in the general direction of Wegger's pontoon.

I kept the torch shining on the pontoon, Wegger was illuminated, plainly visible, and didn't seem to care at this point. He just steered full speed ahead toward the shoreline. The canvas top was now clearly torn and flapping in the wind.

"It looks like he's going to crash into shore at any moment," I shouted back to Tommy.

"He's going to run her aground, probably jump in the woods and hope we don't follow," Tommy said.

A moment later, the pontoon came to an abrupt halt. I shined the torch and watched as Wegger pitched forward. He seemed to land on all fours, but just a moment or two later, he was on his feet and jumping over the railing.

"See that? There he goes," Tommy said, pushing the throttle forward and racing toward the shore. We were almost on top of the pontoon when he suddenly backed off, and we seemed to almost come to a complete stop. He slowly came alongside the pontoon, and I jumped over the railing, bounced off the mangled canvas top, and landed on the deck. A woman, with a number of straps and buckles wrapped around her, looked at me wide-eyed. A white cloth was tied over her mouth, gagging her.

"We're here for you, Chrissy," I said. I had my gun out and hurried past her toward the corner of the pontoon, where Wegger had driven up onto the shore. There were a couple of footprints in the sand, one pretty deep, the other not so much, then nothing. With the jet boat idling behind and now the second boat rumbling in, I couldn't hear anything or anyone moving through the woods. Not that I really wanted to pursue Wegger, anyway. But it would have been nice to know he wasn't aiming at my head.

I hurried over to Chrissy and untied the gag.

"Oh, thank God," she said, then took a deep breath and spat as I tossed the gag onto the deck. It turned out to be a Def Leopard t-shirt. "Is he around? I'm gonna kill the son-of-a-bitch. Are the kids okay?" she asked and then, just as suddenly, broke down into tears.

I began to unbuckle the belts and straps wrapped around her. "Yeah, Chrissy, are you all right? My name is Dev Haskell. Your sister, Bonnie, hired me. We've got the police coming right behind us. The kids are fine. They're safe, Wayne is bringing them back to Bonnie's."

"Wayne? You mean to tell me that idiot's mixed up in this? God, I should have known. Just you wait until I—"

"Don't worry about him, he was with me, we saved the kids, and he's bringing them back to Bonnie while we followed you."

Tommy suddenly hopped aboard, followed by a bald guy with a mustache and some kind of hunting rifle.

"You okay? I'm Pete Byron, Prescott police."

"Yeah, yeah, I think we're fine. Wegger, the guy who was driving this pontoon, jumped off and ran into the woods."

The cop stepped back and turned off the engine on the pontoon. I'd been so jazzed I was unaware it was still running. "I'll alert the proper authorities. Maybe a couple of you guys can help me secure this, just so it doesn't drift back into the river. Then I suggest we back offshore, just to be on the safe side. Ma'am, what's your situation? Are you in need of any emergency attention?"

"I got a sunburn, and I want to kill that bastard."

"I'll consider that as positive," he smiled. "I can bring you back to Prescott, just to be safe. I'm sure this has been traumatic. I'd suggest a night at least under observation. Talking from experience, there's usually a crash once the adrenaline slows down, and you start to collect your thoughts."

"Would it be all right if we brought her back to Afton? It's that much closer to her family and home."

"I can call emergency services and have them meet you. Obviously, they're going to want to talk with you, get a statement, probably ask you some questions. What marina are you out of?"

Tommy gave him his address. We secured the pontoon, helped Chrissy onto the jet boat, and headed upriver. By the time we reached Tommy's house, there was a pretty steady rain coming down. An ambulance was waiting in the driveway, along with a car from the sheriff's department. Chrissy was shivering pretty badly, and what Pete had suggested seemed to be happening. She was starting to collect her thoughts, crashing, and probably should be medicated at least for the night. I gave a quick statement to the Washington County sheriff, then we followed him back to Stillwater. My phone picked up service as we approached Afton, and I called Bonnie and brought her up to date.

By the time I was finished at the sheriff's department giving a statement and being interviewed, the sun was about to come up. Tommy and the other two guys, I never did get their names or, if I did, I'd forgotten, were long gone. I drove Wegger's Cadillac Escalade home and climbed into bed.

Forty-Six

My phone kept ringing, and I had to crawl out of bed, dig it out of the pocket on my jeans to finally answer it. "Yeah," I croaked.

"Where are you?" It was Bonnie.

"What time is it?"

"It's after eleven, I'm at the hospital with Chrissy. We're just waiting for the doctor to come in and release her, then we have to go to the Stillwater Sheriff's department to make a statement."

"Are the kids okay?"

"Yeah, they're fine. A little wild, but they're fine. I brought them to my mom's this morning. How are you?"

"Good, good. If you're there at the hospital, where's Iggy?"

"He's at home, going over the system, making sure everything is okay."

"Is it?"

"Far as I know, yeah."

"Luscious is still watching Iggy?"

"Yes, well, and Morton, and Wayne. Thank God he knocked the power out, otherwise who knows what would have happened?"

"Wayne told you he knocked the power out?"

"Yeah, right after he rescued the kids, he, umm, might have spent the night. I mean, he was tired and all, and after having to fight Wegger and his brother, I just wasn't sure he should be driving."

"I'm going to head over there now. With Wegger out there somewhere on the loose, there's still a slim chance he'll try something."

"Okay, I'm not sure when we'll be home. The doctor has to check out Chrissy, and then like I said, she has to give her statement to the sheriff's department."

"I'll see you when I see you," I said and hung up.

I took a quick shower, more or less woke up, filled a travel mug with coffee, then climbed in Wegger's Escalade and drove over to Bonnie's.

Luscious and Wayne were watching cartoons on the living room couch. Four large pizza delivery boxes were scattered across the coffee table. Wayne's head was tilted back, and he was holding a piece of pizza above his mouth. It dawned on me that maybe that was just the way the guy ate pizza. As the pizza dangled, his eyes rolled toward the top of his head to see who was coming up the stairs.

"Whoa, man, you just getting back now? What'd you do, hitch-hike? Should have called, we could have had your buddy, Luscious, here, drive out there in that piece-of-shit car of yours and give you a lift."

"Thanks for thinking of me, Wayne. Not to worry, I've been back for a while. You know, just tying up some loose ends after you rescued the kids and knocked the power out last night. You tired after kicking the shit out of Niles and Delmar Wegger?"

Wayne's head lurched upward, and he took a huge bite of pizza. He tossed the remainder of the piece back in the box, then proceeded to wipe his hands off on his t-shirt, this one advertised Iggy Pop. "Sorry about that, pal. Guess I just got carried away with the emotion of the moment. Bonnie was so happy to see the kids and all, I didn't want to ruin the fun. I can tell you this much, it worked. I mean, she was really *thankful*. Whoa! I mean, really." He winked, smiled, and flashed both hands, giving me the double thumbs up.

His back was to Luscious, who looked at me suggesting something like 'Just say the word,' then he pounded his fist into the palm of his hand. I shook my head no, then said, "I'm just going to check on Iggy, downstairs. Don't let me interrupt the pizza you guys got."

"Yeah, hey, thanks, good thing they had your credit card on file. Man, that Iggy guy, dude, talk about a fruitcake," Wayne said.

I reconsidered Luscious's offer for a moment, then headed downstairs.

Forty-seven

I knocked on Iggy's door a couple of times before a timid voice from the other side, answered, "Who, who's there?"

"Iggy, it's Dev Haskell. Are you all right?"

I heard the rustle of Mylar just before the door opened. "Well, I see you survived," he said. I noticed he was back to working in the dark, and I wondered if Wayne's appearance had anything to do with that.

"Yes, I'm fine. Thank you. More importantly, any problem with Wegger gaining access?"

"Not that I've been able to discover. Have they captured him yet?"

"If they have, no one has informed me. As far as I know, he is, or was, on foot, and the police are actively searching for him. They have a description, know where his home in town is as well as his place over on the St. Croix. That's where he was planning to gain access to your system, by the way, his place on the St. Croix. It's where we knocked out the power."

"Yes, I heard a version of that tale," Iggy said, sounding skeptical, then he raised his head toward the upper floor and Wayne.

"Don't worry about it. I'm just glad Wegger couldn't get into your system. I should tell you, he had a number of laptops lined up on two desks, and they—"

"How many?"

"Laptops? There were six, all lined up next to one another on a couple of desks. I unplugged all of them and hid them under a couch. Matter of fact, now that I think about it, I don't believe I mentioned that to the police, I should probably let them know."

"I know after Bonnie's report of the kidnapping last night, the police have been at his home here in town," Iggy said. "I'm unable to gain any active access to his system, so I'm pretty sure they've taken everything into custody. They've also received three anonymous reports of child pornography on his system. That program I embedded should have automatically landed on those laptops as well. It's only a matter of time before they realize what they have sitting in front of them. Once they do get hold of him, he's going to be looking at a pretty serious sentence that will essentially mean life without parole."

"Good riddance," I said. "But just to be sure, he didn't gain access, correct?"

"Yes, that's correct. That said, until he's in custody, he remains a danger wherever he is."

"Understood."

"It would be nice to have things return back to a semblance of normal, perhaps have certain parties leave the premises."

"I'll see what I can do on that front."

I left Iggy working on his computer and headed back upstairs.

Wayne was still in front of the flatscreen watching cartoons. Luscious was out on the back deck, eating a large piece of pizza and throwing bits over the railing to Morton down below.

"Hey, Wayne, I'm thinking you'd better head out."

"What the hell for? Oh, let me take a wild guess, you're just jealous of all the action I got last night and—"

"No, I'm just thinking of you. We got the police on their way. They're going to take another statement from me. No doubt, ask some more questions. If I recall, despite your success last night, Bonnie still has that restraining order filed against you. They get here, and you're lying around, they can arrest you. Matter of fact, from what I know, it's against the law for them not to arrest you."

He leaned forward, took a piece of pizza and bit the end off, then tossed it back in the box. I did a quick count, six of the nine pieces had the pointed end bitten off. "When are they coming over?" he said through a mouthful of pizza.

"Actually, they're on their way, but that was about twenty minutes ago. So they should be pulling up in front at any moment."

"No shit, God, why the hell didn't you say something? I gotta get going, man, have Bonnie call me when she gets back. Soon as she ditches that wicked witch of a sister of hers, I'll be back."

"Yeah, I'll be sure to pass that on, Wayne. Always nice talking with you."

"Later, Dude," he said, then hurried down the stairs and out the front door.

"Promise me he's not coming back. The man has absolutely nothing to offer," Luscious said as he walked in from the deck.

"I hope we've seen the last of him, talk about the original bad check. God help me, but I want to throw him off the deck."

Forty-eight

Things more or less quieted down after that. Chrissy was released from the hospital sometime after the noon hour. Once she filed her police report, Bonnie dropped her home, picked up the kids, and things seemed to return to whatever normal is with three kids and a Mom who works. Iggy never did find any breach of their programs. Bonnie asked for and received an extension on returning to Seattle. That gave them three more days, with the weekend, before she flew back there. Wayne had phoned a couple of times, but she seemed to successfully brush him off. I didn't hear so much as a peep from him while she was in Seattle.

I picked her up at the airport Wednesday evening. "So, what's the word?"

"Looks like they're going to go for it. My God, I have to pinch myself to make sure this is all really happening. How are the kids?"

"I think they're doing great. No signs, at least that I can pick up, of any long-term effects from their dealing with Wegger. Your sister was over every day and took them either to her place or your mom's. Iggy seems happy enough, he had the lights off for a couple of days, but they were back on again this morning, at least one or two, anyway. I'd say everyone is doing just fine."

"Any news?"

"News? You mean, Wegger?"

"No, I wanted to know how the Twins were doing. Yes, I mean Wegger, anything happening on that front?"

"About all that's happened is we seem to have more police cars cruising through your neighborhood. That's not a bad thing, by the way, but other than that, nothing. They had his picture in the paper, he and his brother, as well as on the news for two nights. I don't know if that did any good, but maybe someone will spot them. The city impounded his car, the Cadillac, and I sent Luscious over to his house, and the Jaguar was gone. The house was sealed by the police, so I'm guessing they also confiscated his computers. I checked with Iggy just this morning. He's unaware of any activity."

"So I guess that's a good thing," she said.

"Yeah, as far as it goes. Maybe he's too busy being on the run to worry about you and Iggy. On the other hand, I'd feel a lot better knowing he was locked up somewhere."

"Yeah, I guess. You know, they want us out there, in Seattle, Iggy and I."

"For how long?" I asked. I was about at the end of my rope as far as babysitting kids and Iggy.

"They didn't just hint. They stated unequivocally they wanted us out there by month's end."

"Month's end? That's in like three weeks. How long will you have to be there?"

"They're talking about moving us there, Dev. Permanently."

"Three weeks? That's nuts. You'd have to put your house on the market, get J.D. in school, daycare for the kids, find a place to live."

"All of that's already taken care of."

"What?"

"Yeah, they get three appraisals, pay me the average, and buy the house. They're giving us a place to live in for a year, free. I've been through it, and it's gorgeous. I can extend at the end of the year if I need to. They have a number of daycare facilities onsite for the kids. I'm going to look at schools, I mean, it all works."

"What about Iggy?"

"Interesting. How should I say this? They have a number of people like him. They have some socialization programs he can attend, plus they're in the process of establishing a lab for him to work out of. I think I can convince him."

"Tell them to stock up on tinfoil."

"Yeah," she laughed. "I guess what I'm saying is, I don't think I'm going to need your services anymore."

Actually, that was music to my ears. "You sure? Like I said, we still have no idea where Wegger is or what he's planning."

"It's actually too late for him, Dev. Iggy's already been exchanging information, sending programs. Right now, Wegger is just a really bad bump in the road, but it's too late for him to do any harm, at least through us. Listen," she turned sideways in the seat and faced me. "One of the big reasons he's just a bump in the road is because of all you've done for us. I mean, if it wasn't for you, none of this would have happened, or if it did, we'd have our asses sued off once Wegger's little take on things came to light. I don't know how I can thank you."

"Well, you can pay my bill right away, that would help."

"I think I can do that," she said.

I dropped her off, said my goodbyes to Iggy and the kids, then Morton and I drove Luscious home in the Lancer. He was in the backseat with Morton.

"Tell you what, Dev. Maybe you should drop me off at the grocery store. I need to stock up, and there's a Domino's right next door. I could just get a little something to go, you know, just to tide me over until break-fast."

"You sure, Luscious? I feel like, I don't know after we've been together for this long, I kind of feel like I'm just casting you adrift."

"Adrift, Dev? Me, in a grocery store? I don't think so. You just watch the mail for my bill. That's all I need you to do."

"Okay, Luscious, long as you're okay with that, so am I."

I pulled in front of the entrance to the grocery store and stopped. Some guy behind me started to lean on the horn, but as soon as Luscious climbed out and looked at him, the honking stopped, the car reversed into the lot, then quickly drove off the way he came. "Thanks again, Dev. Morton, I'll see you later, boy," he said, then patted Morton on the head.

Morton gave a long whine when Luscious closed the door and headed into the grocery store.

"Relax pal. We're going home to sleep in our own bed the whole night through. No pulling shifts at two in the morning and again at six. No more Wayne. No more talking to computer guys in the dark. We're back to normal, whatever that is."

Forty-nine

I woke up the next morning on the very edge of the bed. Morton was stretched out in the middle of the bed, looking comfortable with his head nestled on the pillow and still sound asleep. I showered, dressed, and was on my second coffee before I heard Morton climb off the bed and stretch. He was downstairs a minute later and walked over to the back door, ready to be let outside. We ate breakfast, then drove down to the office. Louie was at his desk, going over a file.

"Well, the prodigal son returns, and look, he brought Dev along."

"Very funny. How've you been? I wasn't sure if you'd still be in the back room over at The Spot."

"Yeah, that wasn't as bad as it sounds, saved me the walk over there at the end of the day. Cops were by a couple of days ago, dropped off your computer. I guess once you became the big media star, everything was forgiven."

"They find anything?" Even though Iggy had said he'd cleaned it up, you could never be too sure where Wegger was involved.

"You know, they didn't really say, but the fact that you're able to even walk around would suggest you came up clean. So tell me all about it."

We chatted over a couple of cups of coffee. I told him about Wayne, the kids, Chrissy, following Wegger downriver until he ran aground and then disappeared into the woods.

"The guy could be almost anywhere," Louie said.

"I just hope it's somewhere far away." With that, my phone rang. A number came up, but I didn't recognize it. "Haskell Investigations."

"Hi, I'd like to speak to Dev Haskell." It was a soft voice, sexy and sounding vaguely familiar, although I couldn't place it.

"You got him."

"Oh, hi. I wasn't sure if that was you who answered. It's me, Veronica, from the gift shop, in Afton. You came in asking for directions, and then you ditched me later that night at the bar, remember?"

"Yeah, hi, Veronica, I do remember. And for the record, I didn't ditch you. We just had to get going."

"Well, my loss, apparently, I missed out on all the excitement. It's quite the talk all over town."

"Hopefully, it met with your boss' approval."

"Oh, Penny. I'm afraid she's never quite happy, but at least she knows you weren't attending some orgy-fest, as she put it."

"Yeah, does she know you entertain?"

"Ahh, no, that would probably lead to a broken contract. It is how I make enough to buy her out over time, it's funny, in a way. But that's not the reason I called. The town has put together a little celebration for the three, actually four, of you, that is, if you can make it. Sorry for the short notice, but it's tonight. Just a little reception at the bar where you first met Tommy and the guys."

"Tonight?"

"Yeah, it starts at half-past seven. We'd love to see you there if you can make it. Feel free to bring someone."

I took that last statement as a message that she wouldn't be available. "Thanks, I think I can make it. In fact, I'm looking forward to it."

"Oh, wonderful. I'll let people know you're going to be there," she said, then hung up.

"Interested party?" Louie said.

"Not really, the woman who gave me directions to Wegger's in Afton. They're having some big celebration tonight, sounds like it could be kind of fun. I haven't seen the guys I was with on the boat since that night, and hopefully, that cop from Prescott will be there. Anyway, let me see if I can scare up a date," I said, then dialed a number.

"Angie," she answered.

"Hi, Angie, it's Dev, you free to talk?"

"Oh, wow, you're really calling me instead of talking to all those Hollywood guys that are trying to get in touch with you?"

"Very funny."

"I'm glad you're safe. That was a very impressive story in the paper."

"Yeah, thanks, hey, the reason I called is I have to go to this reception or something tonight, and I wondered if you'd care to go with me?"

"A reception?"

I gave her what little information I had. When I finished, she said, "I'll go on two counts."

God! "And they are?"

"We take my car. I'm not really wild about being seen in that pink Lancer thing you drive."

"Okay."

"And I want to be taken out for breakfast in the morning. That Bon Vie place just up the block from you, they have really great breakfasts. I promise you won't be disappointed."

"You talking breakfast?"

"Don't be stupid. I'll plan on picking you up around seven tonight," she said and hung up.

"So?" Louie asked.

"She's thrilled, and she's taking the rest of the day off just to get ready."

"This is the woman who told you that you were unstable?"

"Yeah, and she wanted something more permanent.
I think she's realized her mistake."
Louie just shook his head.

Fifty

ngie picked me up promptly at twenty after seven. I was in the kitchen when she knocked on the front door. It was a fairly warm evening. I had been enjoying a bottle of Finnegan's Hoppy Shepherd and the nice breeze coming through the kitchen windows when the doorbell rang. Morton hurried out of his bed and thundered toward the front door, barking. He gave Angie his usual cold nose greeting between the legs as soon as she stepped inside.

"Whoa, Morton," she half jumped. "Yeah, I missed you, too. You all set, man-of-the-hour?"

"Yeah, look, relax, it's just a few folks and some beers. It's probably not going to be a late night."

"Well, good, because at some point, I want you all to myself. Come on, let's get started," she said then stepped back out to the front porch. It was about a half-hour drive down to Afton, and we chit-chatted idle gossip on the way down. When we pulled onto Main Street, there were all sorts of cars, and my first thought was there must be something going on at one of the churches.

"Dev, I think this is for your deal," Angie said, then turned onto a side street and parked halfway down. She turned off the car, then shifted in the seat to face me. "Hey, Dev. I just want to say, those things I said to you a while back, about needing something a little more stable and a lot more permanent. I may have been a little too quick. I mean, my God, you saved those kids and that woman."

"Relax, forget it, I hear that stuff all the time."

"About saving people?"

"No, the unstable and permanent deal, forget it. Come on, let's go see what's happening. I could do with a beverage." Angie sat in the car for a long moment until I walked around and opened the door for her. She slid out from behind the wheel and gave me a look.

"What?"

"Nothing," she said, then seemed to take a deep breath, "Just thinking. Come on, let's go see what they've got planned for you."

The bar wasn't just crowded. It was jam-packed. There were maybe two dozen folks out in front on the street, sipping glasses of wine or drinking a beer. We made our way inside and slowly headed toward the bar, working our way through the crowd. Eventually, we made it to the bar, then stood there for a good five minutes, trying to get one of the three harried bartenders' attention. I ordered a beer and got a glass of wine for Angie. Before they were delivered, I heard a shrill whistle from the far end of the bar. Veronica, looking like a sultry million bucks, waved at me and motioned me over with a frantic wave of her hand.

"We've got to go join some folks at the end of the bar," I said into Angie's ear.

"What?"

I just gave her the 'follow me sign,' and we attempted to plow our way through the crowd. My beer was just about finished by the time we got to Veronica. Tommy was standing behind her talking to Pete Byron, the cop from Prescott.

"Hey, look what the cat dragged in. Glad you could make it," Tommy said, then slapped me on the back, gave a nod to the bartender, and ordered me another beer. After getting a tongue-twirling kiss from Veronica, I introduced Angie around. She smiled, gave a polite nod as I introduced her, then just stood back, and watched the interaction.

At some point, someone stood on top of the bar and shouted until everyone was quiet. He made a short speech about the town and the good people who lived there. He introduced Tommy and Pete Byron and the other two guys whose names I immediately forgot, once again. He introduced me, but only as an afterthought once Tommy yelled something to him. Over the course of the night, the place gradually thinned out.

I thought we left around ten, but I guess it was really sometime after two. I remember Angie asking if I was okay to walk to the car and then closing my eyes for just a minute once she helped me into the front seat. The next thing I knew, she was shaking me awake and telling me we were at my house.

I offered her a glass of wine in the kitchen, but she said no. I poured myself a beer.

I woke up sometime in the middle of the night, or, rather, Morton woke me. He was standing at the bedroom door, giving off a low, continuous growl — the same constant tone. I listened for what seemed like an hour or two before I finally opened my eyes. Morton glanced at me briefly, then went back to staring at the door.

I rolled over to see if Angie heard him, but she wasn't there. "Morton, knock it off, it's just Angie in the bathroom."

That didn't stop him, and then the bedroom door opened, and Morton suddenly turned, leaped over me to the far side of the bed, and shoved his head under the pillow.

"That's your guard dog?" Niles Wegger said and pointed a pistol at me.

"Figures," a voice said behind him, and then Delmar stepped into the bedroom.

"What the hell are you two doing here? Look, I'm really tired, I got one hell of a hangover in the process of making an appearance. Whatever you think I can fix, I can't. Bonnie's deal is done. You missed your opportunity. You're both in enough trouble after grabbing her kids and her sister. Do yourself a favor, don't make this any worse. Just get the hell out of town before the police find you, and they will, because—"

"Will you please shut up. God, you talk just to hear yourself. Now that you enjoyed your little celebration tonight, you're coming with us," Niles said. "Come on, get your worthless ass out of that bed."

I thought I heard something out in the hallway, and I raised my voice. "Don't do this, your coming in here with a gun is just going to mean more trouble for both of you."

"You've no idea what we have planned for you."

"You're right there," I said as Angie's naked silhouette suddenly stepped into the doorway behind them.

She gave a kick to the middle of Delmar's back, and he folded backward and collapsed onto the bedroom floor. Niles had only begun to turn when she grabbed his arm with the pistol. She took hold of his wrist and twisted, then thrust a fist into his elbow, and I heard a loud crack. Niles screamed and dropped the pistol. Delmar groaned from down on the floor, which earned him a heel kicked directly into his face. As his unconscious head bounced off the floor, she returned her full attention to Niles. Two punches to his throat, a swift kick to the chin, then, as he bounced off the wall, she caught him squarely between the legs. He stood still for a moment, then dropped to his knees and fell forward, face down on the floor.

She reached down and picked up the pistol, then stepped back, breathing heavily. It all happened so fast Morton, and I, were still in bed. "You know these two?"

"The kidnappers," I said.

Fifty-one

We were dressed and drinking coffee at the kitchen counter a little before six. There were still four cops there, all in the kitchen. The paramedics had taken the Wegger brothers to the hospital. Two cops had gone with them.

"I'd guess it's pretty safe to say they'll be going away for a long, long time. Between the kidnappings, the break-in here and at the other place…"

"Bonnie's."

"Yeah, they're pretty much done for. If they ever get out, they'll be very senior citizens," the Sergeant said. "I have to compliment you, ma'am, that was some pretty handy work."

"Thank you," Angie said and smiled.

"Really, you should give me your card. I'd like to check it out."

I figured karate was the last thing he was interested in checking out. We chatted for a while longer. We were both going to the police station later on but in our own time. Gradually, they all left. We walked them to the door. The Sergeant gave Angie his card and asked her to call him about taking some lessons. I wasn't sure what kind of lessons he had in mind.

I closed the door behind them, then watched out the front window as the three squad cars pulled away from the front of the house. "Well, what do you say?" I asked and put my arm around Angie.

"It's been more than interesting, Dev. But I think it's time for me to head home."

"Sure you don't want to rest up before you go?"

"Actually, yeah, I'm real sure. No offense, but taking care of you for the night and then coming out of the bathroom and some idiot is waving a gun around. It's just not my idea of a romantic evening. No hard feelings?"

"No, I guess not, it's just that, well, I thought, after what we talked about and everything last night, you know, you being a little too quick and all."

"Oh, yeah, then you said you hear that stuff all the time and basically implied that you ignore it, that little talk?"

"Yeah, I guess."

"Dev, you can be fun, but, well, I think maybe you should give that woman that whistled at you a call, the redhead. She might be better suited. Look, I should get going, thanks, it's certainly been interesting. Oh," she said at the door. "I'm guessing Morton ate my thong, but if you happen to find it, just toss it."

I watched her pull away, then stared out the window for a long moment, thinking about what she said. When it came right down to it, Angie was right. I should give Veronica a call. I hurried upstairs to find her card.

The End

Thank you for the time, I hope you enjoyed **Foiled**. If you enjoyed the book, please tell your friends and family. Thanks again. My best to you and yours. Mike

Don't miss this sample of the next work of genius in the Dev Haskell series, **What Happens in Vegas...**

Sneak Peek

What Happens in Vegas...

Second Edition

MIKE FARICY

One

Goose was an old hockey buddy of mine, and we'd been deployed together. He'd pulled me out of a firefight along with four other guys in our squad. Fought his way in to help us, and then we fought our way back out. He got a Bronze Star for valor for his effort, although if you ever brought it up, he'd just smile and change the subject. I hadn't seen him for close to five years. He'd bounced around ever since we made it back stateside. Last I heard, he was working construction, but that was obviously out of date.

"I, I gotta be honest, Dev. You're really kind to offer, but it's not like I can pay you. I went out to Vegas about eighteen months ago. My mom was worried about my younger brother, Kenny."

"Kenny's out in Vegas?"

"Yeah, you remember he's got Aspergers. Always had this thing for statistics and numbers, that sort of stuff." He drained his beer, and I signaled Jimmy for another round. We'd been sitting in The Spot for a couple of hours, just catching up with the usual 'Who's doing what to whom' sort of talk. Morton was napping at my feet after devouring a bag of pork rinds.

"He went out to Vegas to seek his fortune. My mom was worried he'd end up with the wrong crowd or, worse, dead. So I went out there with the idea of talking him into coming back home. The next thing I know, I've been out there for a year and a half."

"Is he okay, Kenny? What's he doing out there?"

"He works for one of the casinos, a place called The Palms."

"The Palms? I don't think I've ever heard of it."

"It's a good mile from the strip. I suppose the Bellagio or Caesars would be the closest places, but they're probably a fifteen-minute cab ride away. The Palms has a reputation for being a party place."

"A reputation for being a party place? In Vegas? What the hell does that mean?"

"It can get crazy. Fortunately, Kenny's not involved with any of that. He's in a quiet room all by himself working on numbers and percentages, and loving it."

"So what are you worried about?"

"There are these three guys, a combination of want-to-be made guys and dipshits. They've been trying to buddy up to Kenny, and I can't see anything good coming from it. I was hoping you might have some P.I. connection out in Vegas, maybe put in a good word for me, and I could get them to check these scumbags out."

"I honestly don't know anyone out there, Goose. But I tell you what. I've been getting pressure from a *friend* to take her someplace fun. She didn't really get off on my idea of a weekend in Minneapolis. Maybe a few nights in Vegas would do the trick."

"Man, Dev, that's really nice of you, but like I said, I can't pay you. Tell you the truth, I just don't have the cash."

"I don't recall saying anything about being paid, Goose. Maybe call it payback."

Goose looked the other way, took a quick sip from the fresh pint Jimmy just slid in front of him and changed the subject. "It gets hotter than hell out there in the summer."

"We've been in hot places before, Goose, and we're here to tell about it, thanks to you. I'll get out there, and I don't want to hear another word about it. I owe you, man."

"Dev, I didn't mean you had…"

"Goose, I owe you, enough said. Now, have you been following the lousy year the Twins are having?"

We sat there for another hour, then climbed into my car. Goose was catching a redeye back to Vegas, and I was giving him a lift to the airport.

"You've gotta be kidding me, man. You think this thing's going to make it out to the airport and back?" Goose asked. It was his first introduction to my car. He had just opened the rear door for Morton to climb into the back seat, then tossed his suitcase in.

I couldn't really disagree with him. I was driving a 2010 Ford Escape. The thing had four cylinders, no pickup, the air conditioning didn't work, and the engine had a tendency to just shut down if I pushed it over sixty. If anything, I needed an escape from my Escape.

"Hey, I suppose you could grab a taxi for thirty-five bucks if that would make you feel better. You could walk, but then you'd probably miss your flight. Or you could just shut the hell up," I said, then turned the key in the ignition, and we listened to the engine groan.

"What's that smell?"

"It's just a little exhaust, let's me know the engine's running. Soon as we get moving, I'll put down the windows, and it'll air the place out."

"God."

"I just gotta let the engine warm-up for a minute or two, and we'll get going."

Goose shook his head, then said, "Mind if I ask you something?"

"It was what I could afford at the time, okay? I got a deal, kind of."

"No, I wasn't thinking about this bomb. Matter of fact, I don't want to know any more about your car. You told me once you had a relationship with a mob guy or someone here in town. I can't think of his name, something like Jumbo or Biggie."

"Oh, you mean Tubby Gustafson. Yeah, I sort of know him and try to stay away. We've maybe helped each other out over the past couple of years. I know his main guy, Fat Freddie Zimmerman, too. Pulled his feet away from the fire more than once."

"Perfect. You think they might have some connection out in Vegas? Someone who could maybe help me out?"

"Help you out? You mean with these guys hanging around Kenny? I don't know, I think Tubby pretty much deals with just St. Paul stuff." The last thing I wanted to do was have any interaction with Tubby Gustafson, or, for that matter, Fat Freddy. It never seemed to work in my favor.

"Oh, okay, I was only wondering. There's an ex-cop I work with, heads up security at the Bellagio. I'll see him tomorrow. Maybe I'll just check with him and see if he has any ideas."

"That makes more sense. I think Tubby stays pretty close to home. He's got enough on his plate without going all the way out to Vegas." Bullet dodged, I figured, and pulled away from the curb.

"Hey," Goose coughed. "You think you could find it in your heart to lower the windows I'd like to not be asphyxiated when we pull into the airport."

"Oh, yeah, sorry about that," I said and pushed the buttons to lower the windows.

"What the hell is that red light that just came on the dash?" Goose asked a minute or to later.

"Relax, it's just the check engine light. The thing always comes on after a few minutes."

"You ever think about getting this thing checked out?" Goose sounded worried.

"No, the check engine light just refers to the door locks or the windows or something. Relax, we're almost there," I said. I put my blinker on and began merging onto the exit for the airport. Suddenly, the engine started making a rumbling noise. "Oh, that's not good."

"Oh, Jesus," Goose whined and looked worried.

The engine made a louder sort of rumbling noise, then shut down altogether. I coasted over onto the shoulder of the road, then rolled along for maybe a hundred more yards before we came to a stop.

"Sorry, man, I think you'll have to hoof it from here." We were no more than a block away from the main terminal.

Goose just shook his head, then grabbed his suitcase out of the back seat. "Let me know when you're coming out to Vegas, and Dev…"

"Yeah?"

"Ditch this beast. Good seeing you, man," he said, then started walking along the shoulder of the road toward the main terminal.

I watched Goose slowly walk out of sight, then waited another ten minutes, fired up the Escape, and prayed we'd make it home.

TWO

I was sitting at my desk the following afternoon, looking out the window with my binoculars at the apartment across the street. The girls in the third-floor unit were scurrying around in thongs and hair curlers, getting ready for some event. Both of them were sipping from wine glasses, occasionally eating a cracker with cheese, and in general, just taking their time, which was fine with me, I was enjoying the view.

Apparently, I was a little too focused on the activity across the street. I heard someone clear their throat, and when I turned around Fat Freddy Zimmerman and Tubby Gustafson were already seated in the client chairs on the opposite side of my desk.

"Solving another crime, Haskell, or thinking of committing one?" Tubby said. He tossed a square of chocolate in his mouth and threw the wrapper on my desk.

"Oh, Tub— I mean, Mr. Gustafson, what a nice surprise. How can I help you, gentlemen?"

Fat Freddy looked at Tubby for a long moment until Tubby gave him a nod. "We received an inquiry earlier this afternoon," Freddy said.

"An inquiry? Something I might be able to help you with?"

"We understand you have contacts in Las Vegas, and they've been— inquiring about us?"

"Las Vegas, I haven't been asking anything— Well, I do have a friend out there, an old high school pal and army buddy. He was back here for a couple of days, visiting his mother. We got together, one thing led to another, he asked me to help his brother in a very minor matter, and I haven't been to Vegas in a number of years so I thought I'd go out there, just for a night or two, you know, and—"

"Haskell, you twit, shut the hell up," Tubby yelled. "I don't have the patience for any of your stupid games today, or any other day, for that matter. Now, why in the hell are you having someone ask questions about me out in Las Vegas?"

"Yeah, Haskell. What the hell is that about?" Fat Freddy said and followed up with a sneer.

"I, I didn't tell him to ask any questions about you. Honest, I didn't. He must have somehow put it together that we knew one another, that I had done some work for you and—"

"Done some work for me? You can't be serious. Done some work for me? Did you hear that, Freddy? The last dealing we had was in reference to you lending your car and a gun to that fool who held up my card game. If I recall, my contract with you was something along the lines of letting you live, provided you delivered that idiot to me in twenty-four hours."

"It was forty-eight hours, sir, and—"

"Haskell! There you go again. I guess that's what I get for being generous. More of you putting your nose where it doesn't belong. You think I want people to know I've associated with the likes of you?"

"Well, sir, it's just that—"

"Silencio! You half-wit. All right, here is what you're going to do. In short order, I want your sorry ass out in Las Vegas. You're going to deliver a message, in person, to this idiot friend of yours, telling him to stop asking questions about me. Then you're going to get that numbers-obsessed loon at The Palms, Kenny Gander, to accept my offer." Tubby suddenly groaned to his feet. "And because I'm overly gracious and never seem to learn from my mistakes, you've got until the end of the week, Haskell. The end of the week, or so help me, you'll be hearing from me, and next time I won't be this pleasant."

"What offer? I don't know anything about an offer to Kenny."

"Haskell, so help me. You try and play me for a fool, and I'll have your head. Instead of window-peeking on two naked women drinking wine and eating a cheese ball, I'll have you thrown out of that window." He reached into his suit coat, pulled another foil-wrapped chocolate out, tossed the wrapper at me, the chocolate into his mouth, and stormed out the door.

Fat Freddy stood, gave a shrug, shook his head, and headed out the door.

It dawned on me that I never mentioned Kenny's name. That meant that Tubby was a lot better connected out in Vegas than I ever thought. Goose would have landed around four this morning, probably had a noon shift. And, with the time change, less than three hours later, Tubby's in my office threatening to have me thrown out the window. And by the way, how in the hell did he know I was watching two women, and that they were eating a cheese ball?

I picked up the binoculars and scanned the third-floor apartment across the street. The girls were nowhere to be seen. What remained of the cheese ball sat on the kitchen counter, next to two empty wine glasses. I waited for the next twenty minutes, hoping maybe they were going to return, but neither one of them ever reappeared. Tubby couldn't have an in with them, could he?

I'd have to figure something out fast. That something was going to have to be a trip out to Las Vegas. Not my most favorite place in the world, but then again, Tubby had presented a fairly persuasive argument.

Three

Where to begin . . . Her name was Barbara Millicent Dahl. I called her Barbie. She referred to herself as Barbie Doll. Yeah, the chick with the pink house, the pink car, best friend named Midge, sister named Skipper, and a boyfriend named Ken. I know all about them, Barbie Dahl kept me up to date. Her figure, okay Barbie's, the real person Barbie, was in some ways the result of a skilled plastic surgeon, but who cares? I was enjoying myself, and she seemed to like the attention. In fact, she had just rolled on top of me again. I figured it was probably for another close examination of the surgery, but, hey, I was up for it.

"You really mean it? Oh what a fun adventure I've never been. God, I'll have to get some new outfits."

An hour later, we were having breakfast. Thankfully, the kitchen wasn't painted Barbie pink the way her bedroom was. Even in the dark, I'd had problems trying to get to sleep. This morning we were eating French toast, I'd made it, and my plate was almost overflowing in maple syrup and butter. Barbie had two bites, proclaimed it exquisite, and then pushed her plate away. Not a problem. Besides, I happen to like French toast, so I placed her plate on top of mine and dug in. Barbie, the doll, apparently weighed one hundred and ten pounds, so Barbie, the real-life hottie, kept her weight there, too, no small feat.

"You mean it? I mean, promise you're not kidding. You'll really take me with you to Vegas?"

"Yeah, it will be fun, if you're sure you want to go. I don't want to force you." I shoveled in another forkful of perfectly done French toast. We were eating off of Barbie plates. She had an even dozen of the things, all pink backgrounds with different headshots of Barbie. The one with my French toast featured Barbie holding a little white dog.

Barbie's little white dog, Sugar, suddenly jumped into her lap and barked across the table at me. Past experience had taught me things seemed to go best if I didn't comment where Sugar was concerned. Barbie reached over and took a piece of French toast from the plate, fed it to Sugar, then licked her fingertips suggestively.

"Mmm-mmm, I haven't been out to Vegas for at least ten years," I said. "There's bound to be something new to see in the place. The people-watching is nothing short of bizarre, not to mention all the games. I learned early on I'm the sort of guy everyone wins money from, so it seems to work best if I don't gamble and just watch. Besides, I could use a couple of days off after working on this latest case. I'm in the process of wrapping it up, so, yeah, the timing is almost perfect."

"Oh, I'm so excited, Dev. This is going to be so much fun. Come on," she said, then stood, dropped her pink silk dressing gown onto the floor, took me by the hand and led me back to her pink bedroom.

Four

Louie gave me a look and said, "Vegas? You gotta be kidding. Didn't you tell me more than once how you hated the place?"

"I do, or, well, at least I did, but then I was never out there with Barbie. This could be a whole new experience. Besides, I'm gonna help out a pal for an hour or two."

We were taking a break across the street at The Spot. Well, at least that had been our original intent when we stopped in for one a little after four. It was almost nine now, and neither one of us was feeling any pain. There was a taco special tonight, and Morton was half-asleep on the floor after devouring a couple of the things.

"By the way, you better give your buddy there a walk before you hit the sack tonight, he ate at least a half-dozen of those things."

"I only bought him three," I said.

"Yeah, but then I bought him three, and that couple sitting at the end of the bar earlier, they gave him another one."

I looked down at Morton. His eyes were closed, and I think he was snoring, although I couldn't be sure with the jukebox playing Bob Seger. Morton had licked the plate clean, and I wanted to make sure Mike remembered to put it in the dishwasher instead of back on the shelf in the kitchen. I reached down and grabbed the thing, your basic white ceramic plate, thank God. Nothing pink and no images of a blonde or that little dog. Just a white plate.

"Mike," I said, placing the plate on the bar. "Toss this in the dishwasher."

"Thing looks clean to me." Then he added, "Relax, just kidding."

"Look, I don't mean to pry," Louie said. "But are you sure you're going to be able to travel out there and spend more than a night together without her strangling you? I mean, I know she's enjoyable on some basic level. But a couple of days, you're liable to drive each other crazy."

"She's never been to the place, Vegas. We'll fly out there, stay for a couple of nights, then head back here while we're still on a high note. I mean, what could go wrong?"

Louie looked at me for a long moment, "In Vegas? Gee, nothing. You gotta be kidding me. Just for starters, if you're going to be paying for this trip, give her cash, not your credit card number. She's liable to . . . What's that look for? You didn't—"

"She wanted to surprise me and book the room."

"Dev, there are places out there that run a thousand, no, tens of thousands a night. She could put you into bankruptcy in about sixty seconds."

"She wouldn't do that, I mean, you don't think she'd…God."

"Report the card as stolen or put a hold on it or something. What the hell were you thinking? On second thought, don't answer that, I already know."

"Maybe I should call her?"

"It might be more productive to simply call your credit card company. I'm guessing they have an 800 number on the back of the card. You can get it straightened out in less than five minutes."

The more I thought about it, the more sense Louie seemed to make. "Mike, give us two more. I gotta step outside and make a phone call."

* * *

Fortunately, there'd been no activity on my card. Far from being financially responsible, I suspected Barbie had just been overwhelmed with the options and couldn't make up her mind. By the time we got home, and I took Morton for a walk, a very good idea, by the way, it was too late to call her. I climbed in bed and immediately fell asleep. My cellphone woke me just before five the following morning.

"Hello," I groaned, trying to sound wide awake and failing miserably. Morton had snuck up onto the bed sometime in the middle of the night. He opened one eye and looked at me for a moment, then angled his head under a pillow, took a deep breath, and went back to sleep. "Hello?"

"Dev?"

"Barbie, is everything okay?"

"I hope I didn't wake you." I glanced at the digital clock on the dresser, four fifty-seven.

"Is everything okay?"

"Well, no, I mean, no big deal. Kind of. I found the perfect place for us to stay in Las Vegas, but when I went to make the reservation, I needed the security code for your credit card."

"Security code?" I said and thought, *'you gotta be kidding me.'*

"Yeah, you know, on the back of the card, should be three little numbers. If you can just give it to me, I'll call them back and make the reservations. I was lucky to find four nights somewhere."

That didn't sound right, the four nights deal. It was the end of July, and the average temperature out in Vegas had to be around a hundred-plus degrees. I mean, the place is always busy, but wouldn't the hot summer be something like an off-season?

"Hello, are you there? Can you give me those numbers on the back of your card?"

"Yeah, I suppose, hang on, and I'll grab it." My wallet was on the dresser, right next to the digital that now read four fifty-nine. Fortunately, I'd come awake enough to walk down the hall to the bathroom, then back into the bedroom. "You still there?"

"Yeah, what kept you?"

"I was looking for my credit card. It's not in my wallet," I lied. "It's either at the restaurant where I was in a meeting last night, or I left it at the office."

"Mmm-mmm," she said, not sounding too surprised. "Could you call the restaurant and see? Maybe they could give you the security numbers thingy."

"I don't think anyone will be there at this hour. How about I call you when I have it in my hand?"

"You won't forget?"

"No, I won't forget," I said, and jealousy looked over at Morton, sound asleep with his head buried beneath the pillow.

"Promise?"

I was almost back asleep myself, and I half-groaned, "I promise."

"Okay, call me just as soon as you get it. Bye, bye, bye, bye, bye," she said, sounding all cheery as she hung up.

I switched my cellphone into airplane mode, tossed it on the bedside table, then tried to get comfortable in the little bit of room that Morton had left me. I slept fitfully for the next few hours before I finally got up, stumbled downstairs, and made some coffee. Morton came into the kitchen about an hour later, gave a long stretch, and then waited for me by the back door until I let him out.

I went online, looking for an inexpensive room in Vegas while at the same time trying to figure out how I would explain it to Barbie.

Five

Barbie half-screamed, "You, you already made the reservations?"

We were having a coffee at the Claddagh coffee shop down on West Seventh. People at the tables on either side of us looked over for a moment before returning to their conversations. "Yeah, and I got a pretty good deal. It's a Holiday Inn and—"

"A Holiday Inn?" she said just a little louder than her previous scream.

"Yeah, it's in south Vegas."

"Does that mean it's on the strip?"

"The strip? Well, no, not exactly. See, that's why I got such a good deal. You wanted to be on the strip?"

"God, Dev!" This time when she screamed, there was no 'half' about it.

The woman from behind the cash register walked over and asked, "Is everything all right?"

"Yeah, fine," I said.

"Fine! Are you kidding me?" Barbie looked at the woman for sympathy, "No, it's horrible. We're going to Las Vegas, supposedly for fun, but certain people booked us into a Holiday Inn outside of town."

"Why aren't you staying on the strip?" the woman asked me, then turned and looked at Barbie. "We go out there every year. We always stay at the Bellagio. They've got a great buffet, a wonderful little piano bar where we people-watch, and it has that famous fountain out in front, everybody knows about the Bellagio." She looked down at me and smiled, suggesting I was a no-body and didn't know. "I just love to play the games. I always win."

I doubted that and was about to say something when Barbie's withering glance convinced me it might be better to just remain quiet. "The Bellagio," Barbie said, then looked at me with raised eyebrows.

To be continued...

Where to start, Barbie? Goose? Vegas? Dev will be lucky if he get's out of there for only a hundred bucks. You better grab a copy of **What Happens in Vegas...** I think things are about to get crazy.

Books by Mike Faricy
Crime Fiction Firsts

A boxset of the first four books in four crime fiction series:

Russian Roulette; Dev Haskell series

Welcome; Jack Dillon Dublin Tales series

Corridor Man; Corridor Man series

Reduced Ransom! Hot Shot series

The following titles comprise the Dev Haskell series:

Russian Roulette: Case 1

Mr. Swirlee: Case 2

Bite Me: Case 3

Bombshell: Case 4

Tutti Frutti: Case 5

Last Shot: Case 6

Ting-A-Ling: Case 7

Crickett: Case 8

Bulldog: Case 9

Double Trouble: Case 10

Yellow Ribbon: Case 11

Dog Gone: Case 12

Scam Man: Case 13

Foiled: Case 14

What Happens in Vegas… Case 15

Art Hound: Case 16

The Office: Case 17

Star Struck: Case 18
International Incident: Case 19
Guest From Hell: Case 20
Art Attack: Case 21
Mystery Man: Case 22
Bow-Wow Rescue: Case 23
Cold Case: Case 24
Cash Up Front: Case 25
Dream House: Case 26
Alley Katz: Case 27
The Big Gamble: Case 28
Bad to the Bone: Case 29
Silencio!: Case 30
Surprise, Surprise: Case 31
Hit & Run: Case 32
Suspect Santa: Case 33
P.I. Apprentice: Case 34
Rebel Without a Clue: Case 35

The following titles are Dev Haskell novellas:
Dollhouse
The Dance
Pixie
Fore!
Twinkle Toes
(*a Dev Haskell short story*)

The following are Dev Haskell Boxsets:
Dev Haskell Boxset 1-3
Dev Haskell Boxset 4-6
Dev Haskell Boxset 7-9
Dev Haskell Boxset 10-12
Dev Haskell Boxset 13-15
Dev Haskell Boxset 16-18
Dev Haskell Boxset 19-21
Dev Haskell Boxset 22-24
Dev Haskell Boxset 25-27
Dev Haskell Boxset 28-30
Dev Haskell Boxset 1-7
Dev Haskell Boxset 8-14
Dev Haskell Boxset 15-19
Dev Haskell Boxset 20-24
Dev Haskell Boxset 25-29

The following titles comprise the Jack Dillon Dublin Tales series:
Welcome
Jack Dillon Dublin Tale 1
Sweet Dreams
Jack Dillon Dublin Tale 2
Mirror Mirror
Jack Dillon Dublin Tale 3
Silver Bullet
Jack Dillon Dublin Tale 4
Fair City Blues
Jack Dillon Dublin Tale 5

Spade Work
Jack Dillon Dublin Tale 6
Madeline Missing
Jack Dillon Dublin Tale 7
Mistaken Identity
Jack Dillon Dublin Tale 8
Picture Perfect
Jack Dillon Dublin Tale 9
Dublin Moon
Jack Dillon Dublin Tale 10
Mystery Woman
Jack Dillon Dublin Tale 11
Second Chance
Jack Dillon Dublin Tale 12
Payback Brother
Jack Dillon Dublin Tale 13
The Heist
Jack Dillon Dublin Tale 14
Jewels To Kill For
Jack Dillon Dublin Tale 15
Retirement Scheme
Jack Dillon Dublin Tale 16
The Collector
Jack Dillon Dublin Tale 17

Jack Dillon Dublin Tales Boxsets:
Jack Dillon Dublin Tales 1-3
Jack Dillon Dublin Tales 4-6
Jack Dillon Dublin Tales 1-5

Jack Dillon Dublin Tales 1-7
Jack Dillon Dublin Tales 6-10

The following titles comprise the Hotshot series;
Reduced Ransom! Second Edition
Finders Keepers! Second Edition
Bankers Hours Second Edition
Chow Down Second Edition
Moonlight Dance Academy Second Edition
Irish Dukes (Fight Card Series)
written under the pseudonym Jack Tunney

The following titles comprise the Corridor Man series:
Corridor Man
Corridor Man 2: Opportunity knocks
Corridor Man 3: The Dungeon
Corridor Man 4: Dead End
Corridor Man 5: Finger
Corridor Man 6: Exit Strategy
Corridor Man 7: Trunk Music
Corridor Man 8: Birthday Boy
Corridor Man 9: Boss Man
Corridor Man 10: Bye Bye Bobby

Corridor Man novellas:
Corridor Man: Valentine
Corridor Man: Auditor
Corridor Man: Howling

Corridor Man: Spa Day

The following are Corridor Man Boxsets:
Corridor Man Boxset 1-3
Corridor Man Boxset 1-5
Corridor Man Boxset 6-9

All books are available on Amazon.com
Thank you!

Contact the author:

- Email: mikefaricyauthor@gmail.com
- Twitter: @Mikefaricybooks
- Facebook: Mike Faricy Author
- Website: http://www.mikefaricybooks.com

Published by

MJF Publishing